SURF'S UP

- ◆ MaryJanice Davidson
- ◆ Nina Bangs
- ◆ Janelle Denison

B

BERKLEY SENSATION, NEW YORK

THE BERKLEY PUBLISHING GROUP
Published by the Penguin Group
Penguin Group (USA) Inc.
375 Hudson Street, New York, New York 10014, USA
Penguin Group (Canada), 90 Eglinton Avenue East, Suite 700, Toronto, Ontario M4P 2Y3, Canada
(a division of Pearson Penguin Canada Inc.)
Penguin Books Ltd., 80 Strand, London WC2R 0RL, England
Penguin Group Ireland, 25 St. Stephen's Green, Dublin 2, Ireland (a division of Penguin Books Ltd.)
Penguin Group (Australia), 250 Camberwell Road, Camberwell, Victoria 3124, Australia
(a division of Pearson Australia Group Pty. Ltd.)
Penguin Books India Pvt. Ltd., 11 Community Centre, Panchsheel Park, New Delhi—110 017, India
Penguin Group (NZ), 67 Apollo Drive, Rosedale, North Shore 0632, New Zealand
(a division of Pearson New Zealand Ltd.)
Penguin Books (South Africa) (Pty.) Ltd., 24 Sturdee Avenue, Rosebank, Johannesburg 2196,
South Africa

Penguin Books Ltd., Registered Offices: 80 Strand, London WC2R 0RL, England

This is a work of fiction. Names, characters, places, and incidents either are the product of the authors'
imagination or are used fictitiously, and any resemblance to actual persons, living or dead, business
establishments, events, or locales is entirely coincidental. The publisher does not have any control
over and does not assume any responsibility for author or third-party websites or their content.

SURF'S UP

A Berkley Sensation Book / published by arrangement with the authors

PRINTING HISTORY
Berkley Sensation trade edition / July 2006
Berkley Sensation mass-market edition / May 2009

Contents

HOT AND BOTHERED

Janelle Denison

CHAPTER ◆ ONE

Claire Reissing had five long minutes to wait.

Until then, she carried her cup of coffee out to the open deck and sat down in her favorite padded reclining chair. The unobstructed view she had of the beach was absolutely breathtaking and inspiring. From the white, glistening sand, frothy waves, and clear blue sky, to her gorgeous, drool-worthy neighbor who jogged every morning with his golden retriever at exactly eight A.M.

Yes, the best thing that had come out of Claire Reissing's recent divorce settlement was being awarded the beachfront house on the California coastline in San Diego. Not only was the fully furnished place all hers, but it was thousands of miles from both her lying, cheating ex-husband in New York, and a shallow, superficial way of life she'd grown to hate.

She'd happily traded in sophisticated chic for casual

3

attire, humidity for dry heat, and carefully planned-out days for a spontaneity that made her feel vibrantly alive. She no longer had anyone she had to answer to. Didn't need to get anyone's approval on how she spent her afternoon. She did what she wanted, when she pleased, and experienced no guilt or remorse for enjoying herself.

In other words, she loved everything about her new life. But, admittedly, there were a few things she did miss now that she was single again. Such as male companionship, sex that was for pleasure rather than a sense of duty, and an orgasm that wasn't self-induced. Unfortunately, it had been a very, very long time since she'd been the object of a man's lustful affection or attention. But despite all that, she was still holding out hope that her sixteen months of celibacy would soon come to an end, and that one day she'd experience the kind of hot, uninhibited sex she'd read about in books and magazines.

In the meantime, until Mr. I-want-to-have-hot-mindless-sex-with-you came into her life, she planned to enjoy the object of *her* lustful affections and nightly fantasies. And luckily, she was able to enjoy him daily.

She glanced at her watch impatiently. Three more minutes and counting before the show began.

Having purchased the beach house three years before she'd filed for divorce from Alan, she and her ex-husband had spent many vacations and weekends here in San Diego. Those visits had been enough to learn a few things about her neighbor who lived three houses away from hers. His name was Shea O'Brien and he owned the Irish pub in town, about a mile away, right on the beach. She'd gone there with Alan for appetizers and drinks a few times and Shea, having recognized the two of them, introduced himself.

As a woman, it had been difficult not to notice just how good-looking Shea was. How confident and charming his personality was when he spoke to her. Of obvious Irish descent, his handsome features were enhanced by thick black hair and the richest, greenest eyes she'd ever seen. Eyes that had made her feel a little bit breathless just from looking into them.

He'd been incredibly friendly, but she'd learned during the first few months of being married to Alan that her then-husband didn't like it when she drew attention to herself. Even if it was unintentional, which most of the time it was. So, always the dutiful wife, she'd forced her gaze away from Shea's and let Alan carry the conversation.

The one thing she discovered too late about Alan was that he was a very jealous, possessive man. And even later, at the time in their marriage when it was becoming increasingly clear that he no longer wanted or desired her, it was also equally apparent that he didn't want anyone else to so much as look at her with even the smallest tinge of interest.

During their five years of marriage she'd come to learn that her attorney husband liked to acquire expensive and beautiful things. Like a monstrosity of a home. Rich, elegant, custom-made furnishings. Rare artwork and antiques and high-priced electronic gadgets. The latest, greatest sports car. And a wife he could dress up in sophisticated couture and extravagant jewelry—all in an attempt to make him the envy of his clients and colleagues.

Unfortunately, all those tangible items were easily exchanged or upgraded, and Alan did so often. When he lost interest in his latest purchase, he'd replace it with something newer and better to satisfy his ostentatious nature. So, it had only been a matter of time before he'd grown bored with her and traded Claire in for a gorgeous younger woman he could mold to his ideal expectations.

Claire took a drink of her coffee, remembering the day she found out that Alan was sleeping with another woman, and had been for months. Instead of being devastated by his lies and infidelity, she'd been strangely relieved that their sham of a marriage was finally over and she was free to pursue her own interests and life. Like designing and creating one-of-a-kind pieces of jewelry, and finally having the freedom and confidence to sign a contract with a local jeweler in San Diego to sell her items on a consignment basis.

The sound of a dog barking drew Claire's attention back to the beach. She first caught sight of Shea's retriever, Goldie, as she galloped playfully through the frothy waves breaking on the shore. Then came a full-blown view of the man himself as he stepped down the stairs leading from his deck and headed toward the water.

A giddy sensation settled in Claire's belly and made her heart beat faster in her chest. She knew her reaction was like a schoolgirl with a secret crush, but she just couldn't help herself, especially since Shea had become the leading man who starred in her nightly fantasies. Seeing him half naked was sure to arouse any woman's desires and libido. Even if it was only from a distance.

He wore a pair of dark blue running shorts and nothing else to cover that magnificent body of his. His broad, lightly muscled chest was bare and tanned a warm shade of brown from the sun, and his legs were long and powerful looking. In addition to his daily run, he also surfed regularly, which no doubt helped keep him in shape, too.

And she was reaping the benefits of all that hard work— albeit visually. He was athletic and virile and built like a god. One she wanted to worship in the very worst way.

A soft, wistful sigh escaped her lips.

Once he reached the wet sand, he began jogging along the length of beach, which stretched out for a few miles on either side of their houses. The sun glinted off his skin and the breeze ruffled through his dark, tousled hair, much as her fingers itched to do. As he passed her place, he glanced her way and grinned and waved, as he did every morning. Smiling, she returned the unspoken hello with a wave of her own.

She continued to watch him run with Goldie by his side, until he was nothing more than a stick figure in the far distance and there was nothing left to ogle. Finished with her coffee and her morning's entertainment, she stood and went back inside the house. After washing out her mug, she parked herself on the tall stool in front of the drafting table where she designed her jewelry.

The beach house had an extra room for her to use as an office, but the window faced the front of the house and the driveway. Instead, she'd decided to place the worktable in the corner of the living room where she could glance out the sliding glass door that led to the deck and have an unobstructed view of the beach and ocean at any given time. She couldn't think of a more pleasant, relaxing way to spend her workdays.

Zoey, the gray tabby cat she'd found as a kitten a few years ago and took in as a pet, jumped onto the table and greeted her with a rumbling, precocious meow. Then she promptly laid down on Claire's drawings and rolled onto her back for a belly rub. Laughing, Claire obliged the loveable feline.

But Zoey was a frisky, playful cat, and before long she was back on her feet, batting at a pencil and chasing it across the table until she succeeded in swatting it right off the surface and onto the floor. She jumped down and pounced on the object before it could roll away, and wasn't at all happy when Claire bent down and took the pencil away from her.

"That's my favorite pencil, Zoey-Girl, and I need it to sketch my drawings," Claire said, and placed the writing instrument in a drawer to keep it safe. "You've already lost two others and this is the last one I have like this. Sorry."

Zoey's whiskers twitched indignantly, showing Claire just how miffed she was that her toy had been taken away, no matter the reason. Grinning at the feline's put-out attitude, she tossed a catnip mouse across the hardwood floor, and that was all it took for Zoey to forget about the pencil. The cat went skidding after the toy, lured in by the scent of the intoxicating herbs.

Settling in to work, Claire retrieved a fourteen-karat white gold casting of a pendant she'd designed and poured loose diamonds and gemstones from a pouch onto a velvet-lined tray. She'd recently bought a parcel of gemstones that included tanzanite, garnet, emerald, and all shades of sapphire, including a rare and incredibly expensive Padparadsha. She was saving that two-carat beauty for a gorgeous cocktail ring she'd designed. She was just waiting for the casting to be finished to complete the exquisite treasure.

She spent over three hours securing diamonds and an oval pink sapphire into a simple yet elegant pendant setting. When she was done, she had another unique, custom-made piece ready to take to the jewelers to add to her consignment collection that was already selling very well at the exclusive store.

Lifting her hands over her head, she stretched her stiff back and rolled her shoulders, thinking a leisurely swim sounded good. It was nearly noon, and already it was promising to be a hot June day, which made a dip in the ocean and a bit of sunbathing sound incredibly appealing.

Fifteen minutes later, she was making her way across the sun-warmed sand, wearing a one-piece swimsuit and a large terry towel over her arm.

One of the things she loved about where her house was located was the fact that it was situated in a way that made it difficult for visitors to get to the beach in front of her place, and her neighbors', so there was much more privacy than all the other local, public beaches in the area. With it being a weekday, there were only a few people around— most of whom were lying on lounge chairs and listening to their iPods while soaking up the sun's rays.

Dropping her towel on the sand, she strolled down to the water and kept walking into the ocean despite the initial chill to her skin. Once she was deep enough, she dove into a small approaching wave and swam out a few yards, then back again. Her body quickly adjusted to the temperature of the water as she continued swimming. She dove under another wave, and when she came back up for air, she glanced over her shoulder and realized that she was floating farther and farther away from the shore.

A frisson of panic swept through her, and she immediately started back toward the beach. But instead of making any headway in that direction, for every stroke she made forward, she seemed to drift three feet back. Add to that the waves that were cresting around her and pulling her into what seemed like an inescapable vortex, and she quickly grew tired of fighting the strong current.

Despite how weak her arms and legs were beginning to feel, she fought to stay afloat and yelled toward the shore for help—and ended up with a mouthful of salty water. She coughed and tried again, her voice nothing more than a hoarse croak of sound mingling with the fear rising within her. In the distance she heard the sound of a barking dog, but knew that wasn't going to save her.

She couldn't believe what was happening. She'd finally gotten her life back, and now she was going to drown.

CHAPTER ◆ TWO

Shea piled a heap of shaved turkey breast onto his sandwich, added a second slice of bread, and was just about to take a bite of his lunch when the persistent barking of his dog, Goldie, demanded he find out what had her so excited. She was probably chasing seagulls, which was a favorite pastime of hers.

He headed out onto the deck, intent on calling Goldie in from the beach so she didn't annoy the sun-worshipers out there. But instead of playing with the birds who were scrounging for crumbs of food in the sand, his golden retriever was running anxiously back and forth along the shore, right where the water lapped at her paws.

He whistled for her, loud and sharp, and she stopped and glanced back at him. Normally, she'd immediately obey his command to return home, but this time she didn't.

She resumed her unrelenting barking again, her attention focused on something out in the water.

Frowning, Shea glanced farther out and finally saw the person that was trying to call for help, a good fifty yards out in the ocean. A bobbing head just breaking the surface, and weak attempts to tread water while fighting the current sucking the person out to sea.

Immediately realizing that the person was caught in a riptide, Shea didn't hesitate. He was already in a pair of shorts and a T-shirt, and he quickly kicked off his shoes before vaulting over the deck railing. He hit the sand running.

He dove into the ocean, and thanks to his teenage years spent as a lifeguard, he reached the person in seconds— and was shocked to discover that it was his neighbor, Claire, who'd gotten trapped in the current. Her eyes were filled with terror and she looked exhausted, as though she was barely hanging on.

He wrapped his arm around her midsection so she no longer had to struggle to stay afloat. "Just relax against me and I'll get you back to the beach safely," he said, and was glad when she trusted him enough to let him do all the work, which wasn't always the case when you were trying to save someone in a panic.

With Claire secured in his embrace, he began hauling her limp, buoyant body parallel to the strong channel of water until they were out of danger of the riptide, then started back toward the shore. Once they were there, he lifted her in his arms, carried her to the dry sand, and laid her down, wanting to make sure that she was okay and didn't need CPR or any other type of medical treatment. She rolled to her side, coughing and gasping for air, and he gave her a moment to calm down and get her bearings.

He quickly assessed her stability. At least she was breathing on her own, but he had no doubt she was shaken badly by the incident—as he was, Shea realized. His heart was pounding hard and fast in his chest, and a surge of adrenaline raced through his blood.

Thank God Goldie had found her in time.

Kneeling beside Claire, he reached out and gently pushed wet strands of her golden blond hair away from her face, waiting for her to catch her breath and for her panic to subside. Her cheek was so smooth and soft against his fingertips, as he had always imagined it would be. Despite the gravity of the situation, the attraction he'd always felt toward Claire swelled to the surface in a rush of desire and lust and wanting.

Swallowing hard against those emotions, he reminded himself that she was a married woman. Even if her husband was an arrogant jackass and didn't deserve someone as warm, sweet, and caring as she seemed to be. Caressing her skin for the sheer pleasure of it was strictly off-limits for him.

He blew out a harsh breath, clamped his hands against his thighs so he didn't touch her again, and refocused on what had just happened. "Claire, are you okay?"

"Yes . . . I think so." She glanced up and met his gaze, her vivid blue eyes shining with a wealth of gratitude. "You saved me."

A grin tipped the corner of his mouth. "Technically,

yes, but all the credit actually goes to Goldie," he said, and hooked a finger over his shoulder where his faithful dog was sitting a few feet away from them—panting, but no longer distressed now that Claire was safe. "She's the one who knew something was wrong and kept barking until I came out to see what was up and saw you out there."

She shook her head in confusion. "I don't know what happened. One minute I was swimming close to shore, and the next thing I knew I was being pulled out to sea." She flopped onto her back again and slung her arm over her eyes, the long, lithe length of her body shuddering. "It all happened so fast, and I didn't have the strength to swim back. I honestly thought I was going to drown."

He stared at the rise and fall of her full, firm breasts, and the taut nipples he could clearly see pressing against the stretchy, clinging fabric of her swimsuit. She was wearing a modest black one-piece trimmed in gold that covered more skin than it exposed. But the form-fitting suit definitely showed off her nicely endowed chest, the curve of her waist, the shapely swell of her hips, and those long, slender legs of hers that he'd imagined having wrapped tight around his waist.

He shook that particular fantasy from his head before it got him into trouble. "You were caught in a riptide, which is like a channel of backwash," he explained as he pushed his fingers through his wet hair and away from his face. "When that happens, the current pulls you out into the ocean and is way too strong to swim against."

She lifted her arm from her eyes and frowned up at him. "Then how did you get me out of it?"

"Lifeguard training. We're taught that you always swim parallel to the shore instead of against the current. Eventually, you'll break past the channel of water dragging you out to sea and you can swim back to shore."

She exhaled a shaky breath. "I swim out here all the time, and I had no idea."

"Most people don't know much about riptides." And sometimes it costs them their lives, as Shea knew well from living in the area. "You just need to be careful and more aware of where the currents are."

"You can bet I will be from now on," she said, and struggled to push herself into a sitting position, which seemed to take a whole lot of effort.

He could tell she was still wiped out from her ordeal and knew she'd be more comfortable if she wasn't on public display on the beach. "Come on, let's get you back up to your house."

"Okay," she said with a nod of agreement.

He stood, and helped her up, too. As soon as she was back on her feet, she wobbled and stumbled, her legs still weak and her equilibrium off. Certain she'd never make it back to her place on her own, he settled one of her arms across his shoulders so she could hold onto him, then secured his own arm around her waist and pulled her close to his side. Grabbing her towel from the sand, he guided her up to the house with Goldie following at their side—all too aware of the sensual glide of Claire's hip sliding against his, and the way her fingers clutched the back of his neck.

By the time they reached the stairs leading up to her deck, she was able to walk on her own. He let her go, and she crossed the wooden veranda to an outdoor shower situated in the corner and turned it on.

She glanced back at him as she tested the temperature of the water with her hand. "I don't think I've ever been so covered in sand," she said with a laugh. The fine granules coated her skin from her shoulders all the way down to her feet.

He stopped by a lounge chair and sent her an apologetic grin. "That would be my fault for setting you down on the dry sand once I pulled you out of the water." As for him, it was stuck to his legs from kneeling at her side, and he could feel the uncomfortable scratch of sand beneath his T-shirt from being caught in the current.

Then his own discomfort became a nonissue when Claire stepped beneath the shower spray and unwittingly treated him to an erotic display of pure female sensuality at its finest. He watched in fascination as water flowed down the length of her body, washing away the sand and causing her swimsuit to mold to her curves like a second skin, revealing every nuance of her womanly figure.

When she tipped her head back and lifted her arms to rinse her hair, the graceful arch of her back pushed the generous swells of her breasts out to him like an offering. Her nipples were tight and hard, and the lower part of his anatomy reacted accordingly to the arousing sight.

Shifting on his bare feet, he swore beneath his breath at his lack of control. Christ, she might as well have been naked considering how hard he was getting from just watching, and envying, the tempting way the water sluiced over her slick, wet skin.

He forced himself to glance away and realized Goldie was sitting at his side. Desperately needing some kind of distraction, he gave the dog an affectionate rub on her head along with verbal praise for a job well done.

The shower turned off, and feeling as though he had a better grip on his physical reaction to Claire, he grabbed the towel he'd brought up from the beach and handed it to her.

"Thank you." She dried off her face then smiled at him as she rubbed the towel along her arms. "That felt good. Would you like to rinse off, too?"

He opened his mouth to turn down her offer, but reconsidered. He figured not only could he wash off the drying salt and sand that was making his skin feel tight and itchy, but a cold shower would do him good, too.

"Yeah, I would. Thanks." He stripped off his damp shirt and tossed it over the nearby railing, then turned the cold water on.

He stood beneath the showerhead and winced as the freezing water pounded against his back, which definitely doused any last lingering bit of arousal thrumming through his veins. Suppressing a shiver, he glanced up to find Claire staring at him much like he'd been watching her only minutes before. Her face was flushed, she was biting the corner of her bottom lip, and she had her towel clutched to her breasts. But it was the quick glimpse of what looked like smoldering desire in her eyes that stunned him the most.

"I'll go get you a dry towel," she said, her voice sounding breathless.

Or was the rush of water near his ears distorting what Shea was hearing?

She turned and quickly retreated into the house, leaving him to wonder if he'd imagined the entire heated exchange. He shook his head. Of course he had. Claire had never, ever, looked at him like that before—like she wanted to touch him. Stroke his wet skin with her hands. Maybe even kiss him.

He groaned at his wishful thinking and dipped his entire head beneath the chilling spray.

She returned just as he finished rinsing off. She'd taken the time to wrap one of those sarong things around her waist, which did little to conceal her figure. If anything, it accentuated the sway of her hips as she walked, along with those endlessly long legs. Her hair was beginning to dry into loose, shoulder-length curls that made him want to run his fingers through all that sensual softness.

And then he made the mistake of dropping his gaze to her mouth. Her lips were parted and looked so sweet and moist he ached to close the distance between them and taste her deep inside.

The knot of lust in his stomach tightened, and he took the towel she offered before he did something incredibly stupid. "Thanks." He ruffled the towel over his head and ran it across his bare chest, curious to know where her husband was.

"Is Alan around?" As a topic of conversation, it was a definite buzzkill, and that was exactly what he needed at the moment. Mentioning her spouse put everything back into proper perspective.

She blinked at him. "Excuse me?"

"Alan," he said, just in case she hadn't heard him clearly the first time. "Is he here?"

"Actually, no, he's not," she said softly, and met his gaze with a directness that took him by surprise. "We're divorced."

He stared at her, stunned and unsure how to react to that bit of news. A part of him wanted to punch his fist in the air with a resounding and satisfying *yes*, but he was certain his enthusiasm wasn't an appropriate response for the end to her marriage.

So, instead, he opted to take the safe route with his reply. "I'm sorry," he said, even though his sentiment was a lie. In truth, he couldn't even sum up an ounce of regret that she'd finally dumped her jerk of a husband—a man with an overblown ego and an irritatingly superior attitude. He never could figure out what Claire saw in the guy. "I had no idea the two of you split up."

"No need to be sorry. I'm actually okay with the divorce," she said with a smile that told him she truly had no regrets and was happy with her single status. "Besides, I got this beautiful beach house out of the deal, so I can't complain too much."

Another bombshell he wasn't expecting, but he liked what he was hearing. A whole lot. "So, you're living here now? In San Diego?" Finished with drying off, he hung his damp towel over the deck railing.

She nodded and glanced out toward the ocean. "Yep. It became my permanent home two weeks ago. I've always loved it here, where it's so calm and relaxing. More so than the hectic pace of New York City."

Another ecstatic *yes* resonated through Shea. Now that Claire was unattached and eligible, his mind spun with all sorts of tempting possibilities that involved him and her, together.

He realized that her recent divorce changed the dynamics of their friendship. His strong desire for her was no longer forbidden, and neither was the attraction evident between them. But until he had more time to assess the situation, and Claire's interest, he didn't want to come on too strong, too fast, and risk scaring her off.

"After swallowing half of the ocean, I could use something to help wash the taste of salt water out of my mouth," she said, bringing him back to the present. "How about you?"

"That would be great." And it would also buy him more time with her.

Leaving Goldie out on the deck, he followed Claire into the house. He waited in the living room while she headed into the adjoining kitchen to get them something to drink. Catching sight of a large drafting table tucked into the corner of the room, he strolled over to the workdesk and took in the sketches of a ring spread out on the surface, along with a beautiful pendant set with diamonds and a brilliant pink sapphire.

He picked up the piece, admiring the color and clarity of the oval stone. He was familiar with gems and jewels, and this one was a beauty. Out of nowhere, a gray tabby jumped up onto the table with an engaging meow. She rubbed against his arm and glanced up at him with wide green eyes that begged him for some attention.

He couldn't resist petting the feline, and was rewarded

with a deep, rumbling purr. "Aren't you a friendly thing," he murmured with a grin.

"That's Zoey," Claire said as she came up beside Shea and handed him a glass of iced tea. "And she's a shameless hussy when it comes to getting attention."

After enjoying one last scratch behind her ears, Zoey attacked a crumpled piece of paper and began batting it around with her paws. It tumbled across the table, and she chased after it until it finally fell to the floor. She jumped down and continued playing with her new toy.

Shea chuckled at the cat's exuberance and energy. "She's also very feisty," he said, and took a long drink of the cold iced tea, which felt so good on his dry throat.

"That she is," Claire agreed wryly, and shook her head. "She's always getting into stuff she shouldn't and playing with it."

He redirected his gaze back to the pendant and sketches on the table. "So, you design jewelry?" he guessed.

"Yes. It's something I've done for years as a hobby, and now I'm finally free to make it a business." She paused for a moment, her fingers absently stroking along the condensation gathering on her glass. "I've recently worked out a deal with Seaport Jewelers to commission the pieces I design, and I'm hoping I'll be able to make a living at it."

He got the distinct impression that this was very important to her, beyond making a success of her designs. The hint of insecurity he detected when she'd hesitated made him wonder if her ex-husband had been the one to hold her back from pursing her interest in jewelry design while they were married. Having witnessed Alan's need to keep Claire under his control, Shea wouldn't doubt it at all.

"Well, your talent and creativity speaks for itself," he said, wanting to boost her confidence any way he could. "You do beautiful work with quality stones. That's one gorgeous pink Ceylon sapphire in that pendant you designed."

A fine blond brow arched in surprise. "I'm impressed," she said of his obvious knowledge of gemstones. "What do you know about Ceylon sapphires, let alone a *pink* one?"

He'd spoken without thinking. He hadn't meant to shift the conversation to him, nor had he anticipated her too-direct question that had the ability to unearth a shocking secret lingering in his past. One he had no wish to reveal to Claire. At least not yet. He didn't think they knew one another well enough for him to admit that his father was a jewel thief, or that he'd almost followed in the old man's footsteps. He doubted she was ready to hear that he'd spent time in jail for a foolish attempt to please his parent.

Before he laid himself bare to Claire, they needed time to get to know one another, to build trust between them before he told her about his checkered past. And asked for her understanding and acceptance.

But in the meantime, he had some explaining to do, and he grasped the most logical answer that came to mind. "My father used to collect rare and exotic gemstones," he said with a shrug.

It wasn't a complete fabrication—his father *had* been an expert in acquiring all types of jewels. And in a moment of pure cockiness, and with the foolish hope of gaining his father's admiration, Shea had beat his old man at his own game. His father had definitely been impressed with his son's skills, but that stint had cost Shea in more ways than one, as he'd also been betrayed by the one woman he thought he could trust.

Claire's eyes lit up, obviously delighted they shared a common interest and knowledge of gemstones. "Have you ever heard of a Padparadsha?"

He wasn't above cultivating their common link, however, and he nodded as he set aside his glass of iced tea. "It's a rare and exotic sapphire that combines the three colors of pink, purple, and orange, and it's named after the Sri Lankan lotus flower for its beauty."

"Wow, you really do know your gems." She bit her bottom lip, her features glowing with an alluring combination of enthusiasm and giddy excitement. "Would you believe I have one?"

"You're kidding." Padparadshas weren't easy to come by, and they certainly weren't cheap to purchase.

"I'm very serious. I bought it with a part of my divorce settlement, and I plan on putting the stone in a ring I'm designing. Would you like to see it?"

He found her eagerness endearing, and couldn't help but indulge her. "I'd love to see it." Besides, he was curious to behold such an exquisite jewel up close and personal.

She grinned, and he felt ridiculously pleased that he'd made her so happy. "It's in my safe. I'll be right back."

She disappeared down the hall and returned a minute later with a small velvet pouch. She opened the sack and let the sparkling oval gem fall into her open palm, about a carat and a half in size. "Take a closer look," she urged, and handed him a jeweler's loupe to better inspect the stone.

Picking up the Padparadsha between his fingers, he brought the magnifying lense to his eye and was blown away by the brilliant color and the impeccable clarity of the gem. "Jesus," he breathed in awe. "It's virtually flawless." The stone was just the kind of bauble his father would have loved to have in his collection.

"I know," she said, and laughed, the sound warm and rich and wholly feminine. "It's breathtaking, isn't it?"

"Absolutely stunning." Gently, he dropped the pricey gem back into the palm of her hand so she could slip it into the safety of the velvet pouch. "I'll bet, with the right buyer, it'll fetch you a hefty commission once the ring is designed and the stone is set."

"God, I hope so." She tightened the closure on the small sack, then smiled up at him. "And speaking of commissions, I need to take a shower and get this latest piece I just finished down to the jeweler's. They're expecting the pendant this afternoon."

"And I need to get to the pub." The bar didn't open until four in the afternoon, but he had a pile of paperwork to wade through. "Now that you're settled in here at the house, why don't you come by for a drink and appetizers some time? On the house."

"That would be nice." Her eyes sparkled like the jewel she'd just showed him. "I think I will."

The awareness was back, a slow, undeniable pull he was hard-pressed to resist. When she tipped her head to the side and those loose curls of hers fell across her cheek, he couldn't stop the desire that took hold. Need and restraint collided, shattering the limitations that had always stood between them. And with those restrictions gone, it was easy to finally give free rein to bold and provocative impulses.

Deliberately holding her gaze, he reached out and let his fingers caress the line of her jaw. Gently. Evocatively. In a way that was unmistakably intimate. That touch stripped away emotional barriers and told her without words that he wanted her. In more ways than she could ever imagine.

In response, her eyes darkened to a smoky, arousing shade of blue, exciting him with her ability to recognize and embrace the attraction between them. He stroked his fingers down the side of her neck, and her lips parted with a soft, inviting sigh—and that was all the encouragement he needed to seize the moment.

Sliding his hand through the hair at the nape of her neck, he lowered his head and slid his lips across hers in a warm, sweet kiss. That sensual contact should have been enough to satisfy him, but instead it made him crave much, much more of her. And, surprisingly, it was Claire who opened her mouth beneath his and granted him what he wanted so badly . . . A deeper, hotter taste.

Their tongues touched and tangled, slowly, softly, erotically. A low groan rumbled in her throat, and then he felt her hand on his bare chest—no doubt an instinctive reaction on her part, and one that made his lower body grow stiff and hard. Carnal hunger surged through him, heating his blood and bringing all his senses to life. As did this incredibly responsive woman.

Knowing she wanted him just as much was a heady, thrilling sensation. That insight was also enough for him to end their kiss and give her time to think about their chemistry. Time to realize just how good the two of them could be together. Time to come to the decision to give their attraction a chance and see where it might lead.

Untangling his fingers from the silky fall of her hair, he drew back, which effectively caused her hand to drop to her side, too. She appeared stunned—in a very good way. Like she couldn't quite believe that the two of them could generate so much heat together. Like she was considering coming back for more.

Shea stifled a groan. He needed to get the hell out of there before he forgot all about giving her time and instead gave in to the urge to lift her up onto her drafting table, peel off her swimsuit, and take this encounter to a whole other level of erotic pleasure.

Forcing himself to step away from the temptation she presented, he flashed her a smile, along with a wink. "I'll see you around, Claire."

Then he turned around and left, leaving the next move up to her.

CHAPTER ◆ THREE

Claire checked her appearance one last time in the floor-to-ceiling mirrored closet doors in the master bedroom. Making a statement and catching Shea's attention when she walked into his pub tonight were her ultimate goals. And she was fairly certain she'd accomplish her mission because she looked damn good in her new dress, if she didn't say so herself.

She hadn't seen or talked to Shea in two days. Not since he'd kissed her with such heat and desire and left her aching to feel that amazing mouth of his on more than just her lips. She wasn't avoiding him, but rather she'd been so busy that she hadn't had much free time to herself.

When she'd dropped the pink sapphire pendant off at Seaport Jewelers that afternoon, she'd met with two customers who were interested in commissioning her to design them custom-made pieces. One wanted emerald earrings, and the other wanted a diamond-and-tanzanite bracelet in a unique, floral design. In hopes of making a good impression, she'd spent the past two days sketching different designs. This morning, she'd presented her ideas to the clients and had gotten their approval to proceed with the pieces of jewelry, along with a substantial down payment.

So, tonight was also a celebration for Claire. No more work, just play. Hopefully with Shea. She planned to savor the sweetness of success, revel in her single status, and embrace the sensual woman emerging after five long years of being stifled.

And, oh, was she ever emerging in style, Claire thought with a grin. For tonight's adventure she'd bought a new tank dress with spaghetti straps that was sexy and formfitting and ended mid-thigh. The coral color offset her tan and made her eyes bluer than usual. She'd left her hair down and loose and added gold hoop earrings and three matching bangle bracelets for a little bit of flash. All in all, the look was casual, but flirtatious enough to catch a certain someone's eye.

Zoey strolled into the room, sat down next to where Claire was standing, and surveyed her mistress in the mirror with a very indulgent stare.

"So, what do you think, Zoey-Girl?" Claire asked as she smoothed a hand down the front of her dress, as much to straighten the fabric as to help soothe the nervous sensation in the pit of her stomach.

Zoey gave Claire her approval by rubbing against her leg with a rumbling, affectionate purr.

Claire laughed, which helped to chase away some of her

insecurities. "You're so good for my confidence. Let's hope Shea likes the dress just as much as we do."

She'd never seduced a man in her life, but tonight she was going to try her hand at being a temptress with Shea. His kiss had started a fire in her, one that burned brighter and hotter than anything she'd ever experienced. And that was enough to know that she wanted it all with this man. Mind-numbing pleasure. Slow, steamy, carnal sex. Mutual erotic fantasies fulfilled and explored. A couple of orgasms would be nice, but if it didn't happen she wouldn't hold it against him. She'd never been the orgasmic type—at least not with Alan, or the two men she'd been with before him.

Inhaling a deep, fortifying breath, she slipped into her sandals, then grabbed her purse and a gift she'd bought for Goldie before heading out of the door to proposition Shea O'Brien with a no-holds-barred affair.

She had nothing to lose . . . and so much to gain.

Shea stood behind the brass-and-mahogany bar at O'Brien's, trying to keep his hands and mind busy serving up drinks to the Friday night happy hour customers so he didn't have to come to terms with the possibility that he'd blown his chances with Claire.

Two long, excruciating days had passed without a word from her, and Shea was beginning to suspect that he'd crossed a line he never should have overstepped by kissing her. Hard to believe, considering how soft and warm and eager she'd been with him. But maybe, once he'd left and she'd had time to *think*, she'd decided that she just wasn't ready for a relationship. Either that, or he'd misread the entire situation.

He filled a pint with Killian's Irish Red on tap and turned back to the bar to set the glass in front of the customer who'd ordered the brew. As he started making his next drink for the bar waitress to deliver to a table, his gaze automatically scanned the crowd to make sure that the customers were happy and there weren't any potential problems to handle.

Satisfied that all was running smoothly, he was about to glance away to focus on mixing a cocktail just as he saw Claire enter the pub—alone and looking hotter and sexier than he'd ever seen her before. Judging by the male heads that craned in her direction as she walked by their tables, he wasn't the only guy who noticed the sexy little dress she was wearing that showcased her gorgeous figure, or the way her tousled blond hair made it look as though she'd just tumbled from some man's bed.

He wanted that bed to be *his*, and only his.

From across the room her gaze found and met his, and his pulse sped up a few beats in anticipation. Her pink, glossy lips curved into a smile and she gave him a friendly little wave before taking a seat at a small, vacant table. A waitress took her order and headed back to his end of the bar.

"I need a Cosmo, Shea," she said, and unloaded from her tray the empty beer glasses that needed to be washed.

He'd been expecting the drink she'd always ordered when she'd been with her husband. A nice and safe wine spritzer. He found it intriguing that she was venturing beyond the prim and predictable.

He added the ingredients for a Cosmopolitan in a cocktail shaker and was pouring the drink into a martini glass when a guy came up to the bar and stood in front of Shea.

"I'd like to buy that woman's drink," he said, and pointed toward where Claire was sitting, listening to the Friday night band Shea had hired for weekend entertainment.

She was still alone, thank God. But Shea was certain that wouldn't last for long. Most bars were pickup joints, and O'Brien's had its fair share of men who were looking for a good time. Watching single couples hook up for the night had never bothered Shea before. Then again, he'd never cared about the women who frequented his establishment. Had never been so emotionally invested in one of his customers like he was with Claire.

And that was enough to make him extremely protective about her. "Sorry, but the drink has already been bought."

The other man frowned in disappointment. "By who?"

Shea added a lime twist garnish to the Cosmo. "By me."

The guy eyed him enviously. "Lucky you," he muttered, then walked away.

Shea was hoping he'd get lucky, all right. He turned to the other bartender working for the night, knowing that Mark was more than capable of handling the Friday evening crowd on his own. "Consider me off the clock for the rest of the night. If you need a hand behind the bar, Cal will help you out," he said of the pub's manager, who was on duty.

Mark gave him a quick salute and a grin. "You got it, boss. Have a good time."

Oh, he intended to. He rarely took a night off for himself,

preferring to work the pub and keep up customer relations. But this was one opportunity he wasn't about to pass up.

After ordering a platter of potato skins for an appetizer, he grabbed a cold bottle of Summit Extra Pale Ale for himself, picked up Claire's drink, and made his way across the bar to her small table.

He set the martini glass on a napkin in front of her, a little taken aback by the big rawhide bone with a red bow tied around it that was sitting on the table. "I believe you ordered a Cosmopolitan," he said over the music the band was playing.

She looked up at him in pleasant surprise, captivating him with a dazzling grin. "I did, but I didn't expect the owner to deliver it to me personally. Talk about service."

Smiling back, he shrugged. "Customer satisfaction is what it's all about."

Her laugh was low and husky. "I'll be sure to remember that."

He'd never seen this flirtatious side of Claire's, but he found her lighthearted teasing absolutely irresistible, and arousing as hell. "Mind if I join you?"

"I'd love the company." She waved a hand toward the empty chair across from her.

He sat down, watching as she pursed her lips to take a drink of the pale pink liquid in her glass. She closed her eyes and followed that sip with a long, appreciative *mmm-mmm* that spiraled straight to his groin like a slow, heated caress.

Shifting in his chair, he sought to redirect his thoughts away from Claire's sensual enjoyment of her drink. "What brings you by?" As much as Shea wanted her visit to be all about him, he wasn't ready to assume anything.

She blinked her eyes back open, their depths a soft, mellow shade of blue. Much like he imagined they'd look after enjoying a lazy Sunday morning of sex.

"Actually, there are *three* reasons I'm here." With a smile, she began ticking off each point on her fingers. "One, I believe you invited me. Two, I brought a gift for Goldie to thank her for saving my life the other day. And three, I'm here to celebrate."

So, that explained the rawhide bone, he thought with amusement. Unfortunately, there was nothing specific about *him* in those reasons, but he was still hopeful. "What are you celebrating?"

"Two new jewelry sales." She literally beamed. "Emerald earrings and a diamond-and-tanzanite bracelet." Her voice was infused with pride.

"Good for you." He raised his bottle of beer in a toast to her recent success. "Congratulations, and here's to many more sales."

"Thank you." She clinked the rim of her glass to his bottle, then took a drink.

His gaze fell to the dog treat on the table. "So, you bought Goldie a rawhide bone for helping to save your life. What do I get?" he asked shamelessly.

Crossing both arms on the table in front of her, Claire leaned forward. The position pushed her breasts up, nearly causing them to spill over the top of her dress. "What would you like?"

Talk about a loaded question. He wanted everything she

was willing to give. Maybe even more. And he figured it was time to put his interest in her out in the open and told her so. "I want *you*, Claire."

Her eyes widened. Despite her own brazen question, he'd obviously shocked her with his equally bold and honest answer. She studied him for a moment before asking, "Are you being serious, or are you just flirting with me?"

Holding her bright gaze, he let the awareness between them build and grow before he responded. "I'm as serious as a man can get about a woman."

She dampened her bottom lip with her tongue, the only indication that she was a bit nervous and wasn't nearly as experienced at this sort of thing as she made it seem. But what she lacked in practical application, she more than made up for in effort and pure female sensuality. She had both in abundance.

Lifting her martini glass to her lips, she finished the last of her drink, as if she needed something to bolster her courage to accept his proposition. She inhaled a deep breath, then she smiled across the table at him—a sultry, confident curve of her lips that was as provocative as it was sweet.

"In that case, consider me yours," she said.

A rush of adrenaline shot through Shea. Remaining calm and in his seat was extremely difficult, especially when he had the primal male urge to drag her back to his office and let her make good on her offer right then and there.

Luckily, the arrival of the appetizer he'd ordered kept him from following through on the wicked idea. But despite the interruption, he wasn't about to let her forget her promise, either.

The waitress set the platter on the table, along with small plates. Shea gave the waitress Goldie's rawhide bone and asked her to put the dog treat behind the bar for him. He'd take it home later. Then he and Claire dug into the hot and crispy potato skins.

"I've always been curious. Is O'Brien's a family-owned business?" Claire asked as she smothered her slice of potato skin with sour cream.

Knowing they'd eventually get back to the subject of *them*, he accepted the change of topic for now. "No, it's all mine." And unlike his father, who'd stolen from the rich to amass his fortune, Shea was proud to say that he'd built his business honestly, with long hours and a whole lot of sacrifice. He'd learned the hard way that thieves didn't always prosper in the end. It was a lesson that had undoubtedly saved him from a life of crime.

"Do you have family nearby?"

He swallowed the bite he'd just taken and shook his head. "My mother passed away when I was just a kid, and my father, who'd immigrated to the U.S. when he was twenty-one, moved back to Ireland about seven years ago." Collin O'Brien had settled into a rich, respectable life, with a wife who enjoyed the finer things—including the jewels Shea's old man had managed to heist during his glory days. It had been years since he'd talked to his father—not since he'd failed in the one area his dad had expected him to excel. Shea's inability to follow in his father's footsteps was a huge source of disappointment for Collin O'Brien.

He watched Claire lick off a piece of cheese that was

stuck to her thumb, then reach for another section of the appetizer. "So you come by that Irish heritage of yours legitimately."

He laughed easily. "Half of it, anyway. My mother was English, so the Irish genes have been diluted a bit."

She smiled, looking more relaxed and at ease than she had all evening. "Any siblings?"

"I'm an only child."

Her lovely features lit up in amazement. "Hey, me, too."

It was nice that they had that in common. "Where do your parents live?" he asked curiously. "In New York?"

"No, right now they're overseas in Germany, where my father is stationed in the army." Done with her snack, she wiped her hands on a napkin and pushed her plate away. "I grew up as a military brat, so I've lived in a lot of places."

He digested that information as he finished his beer. "How did you end up in New York?"

"I grew up mostly in small towns, so when I graduated from college, I thought it would be exciting to live in the big city." Her wry tone told him that she'd overestimated the lure of New York City.

"And that's where you met Alan." The music around them was loud, as was the Friday evening crowd, but there was no doubt that Claire had heard his comment . . . and obviously didn't want to talk about her ex.

"Come on, let's dance." She stood up, grabbed his hand, and tugged him toward the throng of people enjoying the evening's entertainment.

As a distraction tactic, Shea had to admit it was very effective, especially since he had the pleasure of watching Claire move to the beat of the music. The floor was crowded, forcing them into close proximity, and she took advantage of that fact as often as possible by brushing up against him in sensual, shimmying movements designed to drive him crazy with wanting her. And he had a feeling that she knew it, too.

Her flirtatious mood returned as she tempted and teased him with her come-hither smiles and infectious laughter. Between dancing and lighthearted conversation with him, she was thoroughly enjoying herself, and he loved watching her let loose and have such a great time. It was yet another side to her that he had never seen before.

The time passed quickly, and after a long set of fast songs she took his hand and led him off the dance floor. Her face was flushed with warmth and she was breathing hard from all the exercise.

"I need some fresh air," she said to him over her shoulder. She grabbed her purse, and he followed her out of the main entrance to the pub's parking lot, which was jampacked with cars.

Outside, it was much quieter and a whole lot cooler.

Walking up to the wooden railing that ran the length of the establishment and also led to the beach below, Claire lifted the hair off the back of her neck and sighed as a light breeze blew across her hot, damp skin. Her eyes closed, and Shea had to resist the urge to step close behind her and feather his fingers along that sensitive spot at her nape.

After a minute or so, she let her hair fall back to her shoulders and turned to face him again, a relaxed smile in place. "I can't remember the last time I had so much fun."

"Then you'll have to come by more often," he said, knowing he'd love having her at the pub on a regular basis. Just to spend as much time with her as possible. "The band is here every weekend."

"The band was great, but you were a big part of the fun. Thanks for dancing with me."

He leaned a hip against the railing next to her and shrugged, though he couldn't stop the grin that tugged at the corner of his mouth. "Like I told you, it's all about customer satisfaction." And satisfying her, in every way imaginable, was his main goal.

An abundance of amusement glimmered in her eyes. "I didn't see you dancing with any of your other customers."

"That's because I didn't want *you* dancing with anyone else." It was the truth, and the reason he'd kept so close to her. "There were guys in there just waiting for me to leave your side for even a second so they could make a move on you."

As if he'd exaggerated, she rolled her eyes. "I *highly* doubt that."

She was so genuinely modest and had no clue how appealing she was. How sensual and alluring she came across in the way she danced and laughed and carried herself. And then there was that sexy dress she was wearing that had turned heads all evening long.

"Are you off for the rest of the night?" she asked curiously. "Or do you have to stay here until closing?"

"Actually, I took the night off."

She tilted her head to the side. "In that case, would you mind walking me home?"

"You walked to the bar?" he asked incredulously, and pushed away from the railing.

"It's not that far, and it was still light out when I arrived so it wasn't a big deal," she said, brushing off his concern. "But I hadn't thought about walking home in the dark, and I'd rather spend the time with you than call a cab. But, if it's a problem—"

"It's not a problem," he insisted. "I walk to work occasionally myself. Would you like to take the sidewalk along the road, or the beach?"

She glanced toward the sound of the ocean in the distance. "How about the beach?"

He gave her a quick nod, and toed off his shoes so they could walk through the sand, glad for the opportunity to prolong his time with her. "The beach it is."

CHAPTER ◆ FOUR

It was a gorgeous night for a stroll, with silvery moonlight streaming across the ocean and the small, breaking waves on the shore adding to the calm and soothing backdrop of sound. Holding her purse in one hand and her sandals in the other, Claire curled her toes into the wet sand, enjoying the cool texture on the soles of her feet, as well as the companionable silence between her and Shea.

It didn't take long for them to arrive in front of her place, and she opened the door with her key then turned toward Shea. The outdoor light she'd left on glinted off his pitch-black hair and illuminated his masculine features. He stared down at her, his green eyes dark and intense, reminding her of the conversation they'd had back at his pub when she'd asked him what he wanted. The one where he'd made his interest in her blatantly clear.

Now that they were completely alone, with a dozen sensual possibilities and this man finally within her grasp, the butterflies in Claire's stomach came back with a vengeance. She had no idea how to go about seducing a man like Shea. A man who was so hot and sexy she felt completely out of her league.

"Would you like to come in for something to drink?" she asked, figuring getting him *inside* the house was a start.

Pushing his fingers into the front pockets of his jeans, he slowly shook his head, though his eyes never left hers. "I'm not thirsty."

"Are you hungry?" The words were out of her mouth before she realized the connotation of her question.

He noticed, too. The playful smile that curved his sensual lips held humor, as well as a trace of something far more incorrigible. "Well, now, that all depends on what you're serving," he murmured huskily, and followed that shameless comment with a slow, visual caress that encompassed her breasts, her hips, and all the way down the length of her legs.

She felt singed by his deliberate perusal. Her pulse tripped all over itself and settled into a steady, aching throb between her thighs. She hadn't planned any of this provocative byplay between them, but she had to admit that the bold exchange made it much easier to put her desire for him out in the open, and gave her the fortitude to go after the affair she wanted with him so badly.

With that in mind, she upped the stakes between them. "I'm serving whatever you're hungry for."

Reaching out, he traced the thin strap of her dress all the way down to the low neckline, then feathered his long, warm fingers over the top swells of her breasts. Slowly. Leisurely. Like a man who had all the time in the world to pleasure her. Her knees went weak at the thought.

"I'm hungry for another kiss," he said in a low, silky tone, arousing her with his suggestive words as much as his thrilling touch. "I'm ravenous for the taste of your skin, the softness of your breasts in my hands, and the taste of them in my mouth. I'm starved for the feel of you warm and willing beneath me."

He paused, letting the erotic scenario play through her head and fuel her own imagination to dizzying heights before he finally said, "Knowing all that, are you sure you still want to offer me something to eat?"

He'd revealed his deepest desires, and he was leaving the ultimate decision of what happened between them tonight up to her. Refusing what Shea was offering wasn't an option, not when she'd fantasized about him doing all those things to her, and a whole lot more.

"I'm sure, because I'm just as hungry as you are," she said, baring her own emotions and sensual longings. "Maybe more so. It's been a long time since someone has wanted me that much."

Heat flared in his eyes and he groaned like a man who'd been shoved over the edge of control. In a whirl of movement he gently pushed her inside the house, closed the door behind them, and backed her up against the nearest wall. Her shoes and purse dropped to the floor as he tangled his fingers in her hair and his mouth came down on hers in a deep, hot kiss that was an aggressive, possessive assault on every one of her senses.

His body pressed hard against hers, branding her with a scorching heat from her aching breasts to her trembling thighs. He shifted his hips and effortlessly wedged a leg between hers. His hard thigh slid higher, exerting a delicious kind of pressure and friction right where she needed it the most. She arched into him, felt the thick, growing length of his erection, tasted their mutual desire as it built, and inhaled the intoxicating scent radiating off his skin—a heady combination of sea air and carnal sin.

Desperate to feel more of him, she tugged his T-shirt from his jeans and pushed her hands underneath the hem. Beneath her flattened palms she felt the muscles in his stomach flex, heard the deep growl of sound that rumbled between them, and reveled in the knowledge that she could affect him on such a purely sexual level.

He kept on kissing her as his large hands drifted down her neck to her shoulders. His fingers slipped beneath the straps of her dress and lowered them down her arms, until her breasts were completely bared. The dress hadn't required a bra, and she was grateful that there was nothing to hinder the immediacy of his touch.

She sighed into his mouth when he cupped her in his palms, gently squeezed her breasts, and dragged his thumbs over her tight, sensitive nipples. Then those strong, skillful hands were traveling lower, following the curve of her hips, gliding over her bottom and down the back of her thighs.

He pulled up the hem of her dress until the stretchy fabric was bunched around her waist.

He ended their kiss, and she shivered when he splayed his hand on her belly and stared into her eyes. Bracing his forearm on the wall behind her, he continued to watch her face, her expression, as he slowly skimmed his hand beneath the waistband of her panties, over her mound, and into the slick, wet heat of her own arousal.

Biting her lower lip, she swallowed back the low, needy moan that rose in her throat. He leaned into her, his hot breath rushing across her cheek as he pushed a finger deep, deep inside her. His thumb found her cleft, and despite how turned on she was and how good his touch felt, she knew better than to expect any fireworks.

But she hadn't anticipated Shea's patience when it came to her pleasure. His sheer determination. His amazing restraint and how much he enjoyed her uninhibited response. The way he stroked her with devastating effect and whispered in her ear all the wicked things he wanted to do to her. He took his time, and was rewarded for his persistence.

When his lips closed over one of her nipples and he sucked her into his warm, wet mouth, her body jolted with a burst of sensation. The tension gathering tighter and tighter within her finally broke on a wave of stunning, unexpected heat and intensity. Her head rolled back against the wall, her eyes closed in surrender, and she moaned and shuddered as she gave herself over to a pulsing orgasm that seemed to go on forever.

She panted, trying to catch her breath. She became

boneless, her surreal climax leaving her weak and pliable. If it weren't for Shea leaning heavily into her, she was certain she'd be in a heap on the floor.

He withdrew his fingers, then removed his hand from her panties. As he nuzzled her neck, he adjusted the hem of her dress back into place. "I guess you needed that," he said, his raspy voice infused with amusement and satisfaction.

"Mmmm. I did." She sighed contentedly, vaguely aware that Shea had covered her breasts back up, too. "Thank you."

"You're welcome," he murmured into her ear. "Though it was my pleasure."

She laughed, and shivered as he placed warm, open-mouthed kisses on her neck. "I believe the pleasure was all *mine*."

He pulled back, a boyish grin canting the corner of his mouth, his eyes bright with his own unquenched desire. "It could be again, if you'd like."

As a lover he was so generous. So giving. So unlike anyone she'd ever been with before. "I'd like that, very much." What sane woman refused the promise of more orgasms? "But I think next time the pleasure should be mutual. Would that be okay with you?" There was nothing subtle about what she was asking—she wanted to make love with him.

"Oh, yeah, that would be more than okay." Then he grew serious, his dark brows creasing in concern. "I meant what I said back at the bar about wanting you, Claire. I think I've wanted you from the first moment I laid eyes on you, no matter how wrong that might have been because you were married at the time. So, I have to ask. Are you sure you're ready for something like this? For us? Together?"

She appreciated his caring, and knew that if she told him she needed more time, he'd back off and give it to her. But that wasn't the case at all. No, she'd waited a long time to find someone like him, and she wasn't about to let this night, or this man and everything he had to offer, slip from her grasp.

Lifting her hand, she placed her open palm on his stubbled cheek and spoke from the heart. "I've never been more sure of anything in my entire life."

He touched his forehead to hers and closed his eyes, a shuddering breath escaping him. "I'm hoping you have protection, because I don't have anything with me. I wasn't expecting to get so lucky tonight."

His tone was laced with humor and hope, and it made her smile. "I have protection in the bedroom." Not because she'd been anticipating this either, but because she hadn't gotten around to cleaning out the nightstand drawers that still held some of Alan's things.

Taking Shea's hand, she led him down the hall, and as soon as they entered the large master suite and she turned on a small light, he came to an abrupt stop. His surprised gaze took in the decor—mainly the floor-to-ceiling mirrored sliding closet doors on either side of the room, and the mirrored canopy over the bed. Wherever you looked, your image was certain to stare back. She'd grown used to the intrusion, though she eventually planned to redecorate the room and replace the current closet doors with something more contemporary.

"Wow," he said as he eyed the bed's reflective canopy with unmistakable male interest. "Someone certainly has a thing for mirrors."

She cringed as she retrieved the box of condoms, and couldn't stop the flush of embarrassment that spread across her cheeks. "It wasn't my idea," she said, making it very clear that she wasn't responsible for the room's hedonistic scheme.

He pulled off his T-shirt and dropped it to the floor, then tipped his head curiously. "You didn't find the mirrors erotic at all?" He unsnapped his jeans and slid the zipper down.

"It was never about *my* pleasure in the bedroom." She set the protection on the nightstand and stared unabashedly as he continued to undress as they talked—proving he was a man who was comfortable with his own nudity. And as a woman, she could easily appreciate such a well-built body. "It was always about Alan and what turned him on."

"*You* should have been more than enough to turn him on." Hooking his fingers into the waistband of his pants, he pushed them off, along with his briefs, and kicked them aside.

"Trust me, that wasn't the case." Without a stitch of clothing on, there was no hiding how aroused Shea still was. Claire's mouth went dry at the sight of his erection, at how hard and thick he was between those powerful thighs. Lust and need pulsed low and deep, and increased in urgency as he stepped behind her, then turned her around to face one of the sliding closet doors so that she was staring at their reflection.

"Then how about we make tonight all about you and

your pleasure, and put these mirrors to good use." Trailing damp, lingering kisses along her shoulder, he slid both straps of her dress down her arms. "Starting with getting you naked."

He accomplished that task with ease, stripping off her dress and panties in a slow, breathtaking seduction—made more provocative because she was watching the whole scene unfold. Once she was as naked as he was, Shea aligned the front of his body against her back, then lifted her arms and hooked them around his neck. Her fingers automatically threaded through the soft hair at the nape of his neck, and her body arched to accommodate the position.

"Keep your hands right where they are," he said, the rule obviously not applying to him since his hands were already caressing her breasts, his fingers plucking at her taut nipples. "Watch me touch you, Claire."

She did, and was stunned by the level of arousal he managed to evoke in her. His splayed hands glided over her ribs, across her stomach, and down to the juncture of her thighs. His tanned skin was a striking contrast to her pale blond curls, and her breath caught in anticipation of his touch.

Flattening one of his hands on her abdomen, he slid the fingers of his other hand lower, delving between the hot, inner folds of her sex. She was still sensitive from her first orgasm, and he seemed to sense that, stroking her clitoris slowly, softly, rhythmically.

The erotic visual images in the mirror mingled with physical sensations that threatened to overwhelm her. The reflection of her and Shea together, of what he was doing to her, was too carnal. Too stimulating. Too wicked and wanton.

Unable to stop herself, she knotted her fingers in his hair and moved her hips restlessly against the heated length of his shaft, which was pressing insistently against her bottom. She heard him groan like a man in pain, felt the clutch and pull of his hand on her stomach as he drew her backside closer and pushed his fingers deeper inside her so it felt as though he was taking her from behind.

She didn't think it was possible, but she was going to come again. She turned her head and sought his mouth, and he gave her the kind of kiss she craved. It was hot and wet and wild—just like the unrestrained climax that convulsed through her.

She barely had a chance to recover before he was guiding her onto the middle of the bed. Obviously done with foreplay, he sheathed himself with a condom, then moved over her and kneed her legs wide apart so he could settle in between her trembling thighs. His features were taut, the muscles across his shoulders bunching with barely concealed control, and his eyes blazing with need. Bracing his arms on either side of her head, he crushed his mouth to hers and slid the head of his shaft along her soft folds of flesh, then nudged slowly inside her body.

He was hot and hard and huge, the size and strength of him making her head spin and her inner muscles clench involuntarily. Even though she was plenty wet, it took a couple of pushes for him to get farther inside, and even then it wasn't enough. He hooked one of her legs over his hip, thrust high and hard, and slid in deeper, then deeper still.

She gasped at the burning sensation, at the heat and friction gathering within her. Within seconds, the discomfort gradually ebbed into a luxurious kind of pleasure, and she instinctively arched into him, making him groan as she took more of him. All of him.

He ended the kiss and grazed his warm, damp lips across her cheek. "Look up, Claire," he ordered huskily. "Look at the two of us together."

Her gaze automatically went to the mirrored canopy, taking in their entangled bodies, the clutch of her fingers against his muscled back, and the slide of her hands down the slope of his spine. She watched the way his buttocks tightened and flexed with each thrust and retreat, and knew she'd never be able to look into the mirror above her without thinking of this amazing moment with Shea.

He lifted his head and looked deep into her eyes—as if he could see all the way to her soul. She'd never felt so full before—physically and emotionally. This man had a way of knowing just what she needed, and he gave it to her unselfishly, including an all-consuming passion she never realized existed until him. Now it was his turn to let go, and she made it impossible for him to hold back any longer.

Wrapping both of her legs high around his waist, she pulled his hips down with her heels and squeezed him tight, over and over again. With a low, rough growl, he tossed his head back, pumped into her one last time, and abandoned himself to his own shattering orgasm.

"I have a confession to make."

Shea glanced at Claire, who was sitting next to him on her deck the next morning, looking extremely sated and relaxed. They'd just eaten the omelettes and fruit she'd made for breakfast, and were now enjoying each other's company, the cool breeze, and the view of the calm, clear ocean.

Shea had to admit it was a great way to spend a Saturday morning.

Her offhand comment definitely intrigued him, and he couldn't wait to hear what she had to say. "Okay, let's hear it."

She wrapped both of her hands around her coffee mug, the pink glow of her complexion a result of her sheepish admission and a night of great sex. "Promise you won't laugh?"

He strove for a very serious expression, but knew he couldn't completely hide his amusement, or his curiosity. "I promise," he said solemnly.

"I look forward to you jogging every morning." She set her coffee mug on the glass table and tucked her loose hair behind her ear, her blush deepening. "I know it's silly, and very girlish, but I sit out on my deck a few minutes before eight and I wait until you come out of your house and run by mine with Goldie. Seeing you every morning has been the best part of my day."

He smiled, and couldn't resist picking up her hand and threading his fingers through hers. "Then I guess I should tell you that I made it a point of jogging at exactly eight in hopes of seeing *you*."

She tipped her head back and burst out laughing, the sound infectious and carefree.

He tried to look indignant. "Hey, you laughed."

"*I* never promised I wouldn't." Grinning, she rested her head against the lounge chair, her blue eyes softening with affection. "I can't believe I'm saying this, but I'm glad I got caught in that current."

"Going to such extremes wasn't necessary to get my attention." Not when he'd noticed Claire the first time he'd laid eyes on her.

"Maybe not, but it helped speed up the process of us getting together."

"Okay, I'll give you that." Still holding her hand, he absently stroked his thumb across the center of her palm. "Are you going to be busy today?"

Her eyes lit up with excitement. "Actually, I'm picking up the casting for the Padparadsha ring today, so I'll probably get started on the setting."

He gave her fingers an encouraging squeeze. "I can't wait to see what it looks like once it's finished."

"Me, too. It's going to be amazing." She curled her legs beneath her on the chair. "What are you doing today?"

"I've got weekly inventory to do, and deliveries at the pub. It's my Saturday routine," he told her, then glanced at his watch. "In fact, as much as I hate to leave, I have a delivery in about forty minutes, and I need to be there when it arrives."

He stood, and she glanced up at him, a soft sigh of disappointment on her lips. "I guess all good things have to come to an end, don't they?"

Bracing his hands on the arms of her chair, he leaned in close. "Not us. Last night was just the beginning, Claire." And just in case she had any niggling doubts in that pretty head of hers, he lowered his mouth to hers and engaged her in a long, soft, sensual kiss that started as a promise, and grew into a restless kind of hunger.

Before he said to hell with inventory and deliveries and spent the day in Claire's bed, he lifted his head and ended the kiss. "How about dinner at my place tonight?" And after a good meal, they could finish where they'd just left off.

She nodded. "Yeah, I'd like that."

He could hardly wait to be with her again.

CHAPTER ◆ FIVE

Claire didn't think it was possible to feel so happy and content, and it had nothing to do with the fabulous dinner Shea had cooked up for her, and everything to do with enjoying her new life and this man who made her laugh and smile more than she had in the past five years. Add to that his interest in her jewelry designs, and his support, and she was beginning to think that she could open up her heart and trust a man again. More specifically, Shea.

Claire helped Shea clean up the kitchen, then he poured them each a glass of wine, grabbed a blanket, and they walked down to the beach with Goldie as dusk settled in. It had been a beautiful summer afternoon, and in Claire's opinion enjoying the last of the sun setting over the horizon with Shea was a perfect ending to the day.

Finding a nice, flat spot, Shea spread open the blanket and they sat down side by side. Goldie found a spot on the sand and made herself comfortable. As they watched, the sun dipped slowly toward what looked like the end of the ocean, casting rich hues of pink, orange, and red across the sky.

"Claire, there's something I've been wanting to ask you," Shea said, pulling her attention from the glorious view. "But it might be a sensitive subject."

He looked so serious and direct, she couldn't imagine what had changed his mood so drastically. "Okay," she said cautiously, because she had no idea what she was agreeing to.

"Why did you and Alan divorce?"

As far as sensitive topics went, his question was a zinger. It demanded personal and private answers, and while she'd managed to avoid discussing Alan when Shea had asked about him last night at the pub, there was no escaping Shea—or the question—now.

Then again, hadn't she just made the conscious decision to open her heart and trust again? Sharing intimate details of her marriage, and her divorce, was certainly a start—no matter how unpleasant the topic.

She took a drink of her wine, then set the glass aside in the sand and buried the stem so it didn't tip over. "Well, finding out that your husband has been lying and cheating and sleeping with another woman tends to put a damper on a marriage."

He winced. "I take it you caught him?"

Drawing her knees up, she wrapped her arms around her legs, her gaze focused on the last bit of sun setting over the horizon as she thought back to the moment she'd discovered Alan's infidelity. "For months I suspected that something was going on. He was working a lot of late nights at the office, except when I called he never answered his phone. I tried his cell, and if I did get through to him he was always very short and abrupt with me. He was also gone at least two weekends of the month on what he called a business trip."

"Sounds like all the classic signs of an affair to me," Shea said, and sipped his wine.

She nodded. "And I knew that, but I had no actual proof until I found a receipt in his coat pocket for a hotel in New York City. Considering that he worked in the city, there was absolutely no reason he needed to stay in a hotel there unless he was seeing someone on the side."

"You know, I don't understand why spouses cheat," Shea said, disgust lacing his tone. "If they aren't happy in the marriage, why not just get out of it instead of having an affair?"

It was a rhetorical question, but she'd always felt the same way. "I'm sure sooner or later Alan would have asked me for a divorce. It was just a matter of time, and when I confronted him with what I'd found in his coat pocket, it made it easy for him to come clean and admit that he wanted to end our marriage."

"That must have hurt," Shea said, his voice gruff with a dose of anger on her behalf.

Yes, the lies and deceit had stung because no wife wanted to discover that her husband was sleeping with another woman. The realization that she hadn't been enough for Alan had been painful and had definitely left her with her share of insecurities. But she was rebuilding her life and confidence the best she could, and Shea was responsible for a good part of that, too.

"I had known the marriage was over for a while," she admitted to Shea. "Alan was distant, sex was nearly non-existent, and whenever I brought up the subject of starting a family, he'd put me off with excuses. In that, at least, he did me a huge favor. The last thing I'd want to put a child through is a divorce."

"I'm sorry you had to go through all that crap," he said softly, compassionately.

She flashed him a fabricated smile, but knew that he'd see right through her attempt to make light of things. "You know what they say. What doesn't kill you makes you stronger."

He studied her for a long moment as he reached over to Goldie and leisurely stroked her fur coat. "Why did you marry him, Claire?" he finally asked.

"I loved him," she answered honestly. "Or else I never would have married him."

"I believe you." He finished his wine and added his glass next to hers in the sand. "I guess what I should have asked is what attracted you to him."

She frowned, unsure what Shea was getting at. "Why do you ask?"

"Because I knew from the first time I met Alan that he was a conceited, pompous jerk," Shea stated bluntly. "And I couldn't help but wonder what you saw in Alan to marry him. Now that I know you better, I'm even more curious."

Her stomach twisted, because the question made her

take a good hard look at the reasons why she'd fallen for Alan, and she knew she might not like her own answers. But as difficult as that might be, she saw this opportunity as a chance to purge herself of the past and start out fresh with Shea.

"I was twenty-three when I met Alan, and now that I look back, I can see that I was much too young and impressionable." Hopeful and trusting, too. "He came into the jewelry store where I was working in New York City, looking to buy a gift for his mother's birthday."

"Is that how you became interested in gems and jewelry design? Working in a jewelry store?" Shea guessed.

"Yes." Except she'd given up those dreams when she'd gotten married, because Alan hadn't wanted her to work at all. "Anyway, Alan was very charming and had a way of making me feel beautiful and special. He pursued me like no other man ever had. He sent me flowers and took me on weekend getaways and literally spoiled me. He was seven years older than me, an established attorney in a prominent law firm, and he made it so easy for me to get caught up in his persistent courtship and fall for him. So, when he asked me to marry him, I honestly thought I'd found my happily-ever-after."

"I hear a 'but' in there somewhere."

"Of course you do, or I wouldn't be divorced," she said humorously. "About six months after we were married, I started seeing a different side to Alan. I always knew that he liked buying and collecting nice, expensive things, but it seemed to be an obsession with him. He spent money on antiques and artwork, and imported cars and things for the house. He even bought me designer clothing to wear and extravagant jewelry."

He grinned wryly. "What woman wouldn't like that?"

"Sure, it was nice for a while because I grew up with parents who lived a modest life, but after a while it felt suffocating because it was all so excessive." A cool evening breeze blew across the beach, and Claire shivered and hugged her knees tighter to her chest. "Alan always expected me to look the height of sophistication, and he was also extremely jealous and possessive, which was difficult to deal with, too."

Shea moved silently behind her on the blanket, so that she was sitting between his widespread legs. Tucking his arms around her waist, he pulled her back to his chest and she instinctively leaned against him, his body heat surrounding her, warming her.

He buried his face in her hair and breathed deeply. "Go on, I'm still listening."

"Over the years Alan and I were married, I watched him exchange and upgrade to the latest and greatest," she continued. "And I realized that Alan had this compulsion to be surrounded by beautiful, expensive things. It was the competitive nature in him, and he liked looking like a hotshot with his friends and colleagues."

"That's the man I saw, too," Shea said.

"I guess I saw it too late." She snuggled closer to him, marveling at how safe he made her feel, how secure. Letting down her guard with Shea, in all ways, was proving to be incredibly easy to do. "I'm a simple girl at heart, and

I've never needed much to make me happy. Certainly not material things, and that's what mattered to Alan."

She swallowed the knot in her throat; this next part wasn't easy for her to admit out loud. "Somewhere along the way, Alan grew bored with me, and like everything else in his life, he wanted someone younger and more beautiful to adorn his arm. In with the new and out with the old, as they say."

"Oh, yeah, twenty-eight is ancient," he said, and tickled her until she laughed and squirmed in his arms. "The way I see things, it's Alan's loss, and my gain."

She smiled to herself, liking the way that sounded. "I'm okay with everything, even the divorce. I think the worst part of the entire ordeal was being lied to and deceived. Especially when you trust someone so completely, only to find out that they aren't who you thought they were. It makes you feel like a fool."

Behind her, she felt Shea stiffen, and wondered what she'd said to prompt such a reaction.

"Claire . . ." Her name sounded hoarse, as if he was having trouble speaking.

Turning in his arms, she looked up at him, seeing shades of turmoil in his gaze. "Shea, what's wrong?"

"There's something—"

The shrill ring of a cell phone interrupted whatever he'd been about to say. Cursing beneath his breath, he shifted and unclipped his cell from the waistband of his pants. After a quick glance at the caller ID, he answered the unit.

"What's up, Cal?" he said, then mouthed to Claire, "It's my bar manager."

Sensing the call was important, she moved away to give him space. Shea's brows creased in concern as he listened intently to whatever Cal was saying.

"Christ," he muttered after a minute had passed, and dragged a hand through his hair. "I'll be right in."

He snapped the phone shut and was on his feet, then helped Claire stand, too. "I'm sorry to cut the evening short, but I need to get to the pub. My bartender, Mark, was washing a glass and it broke in his hand. He cut himself pretty badly, and Cal needs to get him to the hospital for stitches."

She completely understood, and picked up their wineglasses while he gathered up the blanket. Whatever had been on his mind would have to wait.

They headed back to his house so Shea could grab his car keys. He drove to her place first to drop her off.

"How about I come by later, if that's okay with you?" he asked.

"I'd like that. I'll be working on my Padparadsha ring." Now that she had the setting, she was anxious to put it all together.

"Good." He gave her a quick, hard kiss that only whet her appetite for more, then pulled back. "Wait up for me. I'll make it worth your while." He winked at her.

She laughed and dragged a finger down the middle of his chest. "Maybe I'll make it worth *your* while," she teased right back.

His eyes darkened with heat and anticipation. "Now there's an offer I'm not about to refuse."

It was after ten at night when Cal finally returned from the hospital and Shea was able to leave O'Brien's. He headed straight to Claire's, her sultry promise still ringing in his head. Her parting remark to him had fueled his fantasies and kept him running on adrenaline all night long.

She opened her front door wearing a silky thigh-length robe, and something equally silky and sexy beneath, and let him in. "How's Mark?"

"He ended up with six stitches right below his thumb on his left hand," Shea said, as he followed her into the living room where she'd been working on her jewelry.

She cringed. "That sounds painful."

"Mark's a tough guy. He'll be out for a few days, but he'll be fine."

"That's good to hear." Taking his hand, she led him over to the drafting table, where Zoey was curled up in the corner taking a nap while Claire worked. The feline awoke, looked up at him, blinked languidly, then went right back to sleep again.

It was the first time he'd seen the normally energetic and mischievous Zoey be so lazy.

"Look what I've gotten done." Claire lifted the gold setting to the bright light over the table, giving him a good look at the dazzling princess-cut diamonds she'd mounted down the side of the ring. The stones were perfectly aligned and beautifully showcased in a channel-type setting.

"You've been busy," he said with a grin.

"I still need to set the Padparadsha, of course." Using jewelry tweezers, she picked up the expensive gemstone and held it against the center prongs, giving him an idea of what the finished product would look like. "What do you think?"

"I think it's going to be amazing." He slipped his arms around her waist from behind and untied the sash around her waist, his mouth inches from her ear. "Just like you are."

She placed the brilliant sapphire back on the velvet pouch on the table, then turned around in his embrace, her robe gaping open to reveal a low-cut, lace-trimmed teddy that was sexy as hell. "You don't need to flatter me to get lucky."

God, she was beautiful, and he was already hard with wanting her. "It's not flattery, sweetheart," he said as he brushed his knuckles across the upper swells of her breasts, which caused her nipples to tighten against the pale pink silk. "It's the absolute truth."

Her eyes blazed with pure temptation as she flattened her hands on his chest, curled her fingers into his cotton T-shirt, and gave it a playful tug. "I'm about two seconds away from ripping off your clothes and taking advantage of you."

That's all Shea needed to hear to take Claire into the bedroom so she could have her way with him, and he had her there in record time. She shrugged out of her robe as he yanked his T-shirt over his head, then took off his shoes and socks. She shimmied out of her panties, and he went for the fastening on his jeans, but she stepped close and pushed his hands away before he had the chance to get them undone.

Her fingers toyed with the top button before skimming down the length of his fly. Brazenly, she cradled his fierce erection in her palm and gently nipped at his lower lip with her teeth. "*I* want to take off your jeans," she said as she stroked him slowly through the denim.

Groaning at the snug fit of her hand squeezing his shaft, and the aggressive way she was taking control of tonight's seduction, he relinquished the task to her.

She unbuttoned his pants, slid the zipper down over his bulge, then slipped her hands under the waistband and pushed his jeans and briefs down to his thighs. His thick, aching cock sprang free, and she touched him lightly, briefly—just enough to tempt and tease and cause the fire in his groin to surge hotter—before pushing him backward a few steps until he was sitting on the bed. She knelt in front of him, removed the last of his clothes, then pushed his knees wide apart so she could move in between.

She looked up at him, licked her lips, and skimmed her cool hands up his thighs until she held the most masculine part of him in her hands. Her thumb traced the throbbing vein leading up to the swollen tip, and he sucked in a sharp, unexpected breath when her finger slipped through the slick moisture gathering there and rubbed it over and around the sensitive head.

Then, lashes falling to half-mast, she leaned into him and trailed soft, hot kisses along his chest, lapping her tongue over each of his taut nipples. His pulsing shaft was nestled between the pillow of her breasts and rubbed sensually against the silk of her teddy whenever she moved. Between the damp lips gradually making their way lower, and the erotic, mind-blowing sensations against his cock, he thought he'd died and gone to the sweetest kind of heaven.

But that pleasure was nothing compared to the soft, wet warmth of her mouth enveloping him, the swirling caress of her tongue, and the suctioning pull threatening to make him erupt. Added to that, he dared to look into the mirrored closet door across from the bed, dared to watch his private liaison with Claire play out like their own steamy, X-rated flick.

He let himself enjoy her ministrations as long as he could without coming, but could feel the need quickly cresting beyond his control. Wanting to be buried deep inside her when he climaxed, he speared his fingers through her hair and gently eased her away.

"I need a condom," he rasped, and she opened the nightstand drawer and gave him one.

Quickly and efficiently, he rolled on the protection, but before he could take charge and drag her beneath him, she was pressing him back on the bed and crawling over him on all fours. Her hands were braced on either side of his shoulders and her knees were pressed against his hips— the only part of her that was touching him. With a come-hither look in her eyes, and her silk teddy skimming her curves, she looked like a sexy nymph from his wildest dreams.

Except everything about this woman was real. Her allure. Her passion. Her hunger. And it was all for him.

He reached down and slid his hand between her open thighs, finding her warm and creamy and turned on, just from pleasuring him. Absolutely incredible, he thought, and stroked her intimately, deeply, just to heighten sensations and coax her closer to orgasm. Before long, her blue eyes glazed with desire, her lips parted on a soft moan, and her fingers clutched at the covers on the bed beside him.

She was ready, and so was he.

Skimming his hands up the back of her thighs, he grabbed the hem of her teddy and pulled it up and off of her, so that she was just as naked as he was. He caressed her breasts, lightly pinched her nipples until she gasped, then took her waist in his hands and guided her down until the tip of his shaft penetrated the entrance to her body. He slid in an inch, felt her clench around him, and left the rest up to her.

"Take me, Claire," he urged huskily. "Take *all* of me."

Flattening her hands on his belly, she dropped her head back with a breathy, arousing purr of sound as she pushed down, accepting every inch he had to give, until she was finally, completely, seated on his cock and he had no idea where he left off and she began.

Then she started to move, her hips rocking and gyrating against him, on top of him, in a slow, uninhibited lap dance that pulled him deeper with each roll of her hips. She arched into him, took her own breasts in her hands, and pleasured herself while he watched.

The provocative sight shoved him toward that fine edge

of restraint, and he instinctively drove his hips higher, harder, in counterpart to her languid thrusts. His entire body shuddered as she continued to ride him, his eyes rolled back, and a low growl rumbled up from his throat. She felt so fucking good, so hot and tight. A perfect fit in every way.

She completed him in a way no other woman had.

It was the last coherent thought he had as Claire started to come, her soft moans and the frenzied movements of her hips triggering his own powerful orgasm.

CHAPTER ◆ SIX

After an incredible night of sex with Shea, Claire was surprised, and disappointed, to wake up in bed alone. She was also shocked to discover that it was nearly eight-thirty in the morning, which was late for her. Then again, Shea *had* kept her up most of the night, exhausting her with his stamina, until she'd finally fallen asleep against his warm body with her head on his chest and his heart beating a steady cadence in her ear.

Smiling at the memories, she slipped out of bed and put on her robe, hoping that Shea was still there. The living room was empty, and she opened the sliding glass door and checked out on the deck, only to find that vacant, too. Bummed that he'd left so early, and while she was asleep, no less, she headed back into the kitchen to make some coffee. A handwritten note on the counter caught her attention, and she picked up the piece of paper and read Shea's message.

You were sleeping so peacefully and I didn't want to wake you. The waves were perfect for surfing this morning and I couldn't resist. Sorry I won't be there for my daily jog, but I promise to make it up to you later. Shea.

Relieved that she hadn't done something to scare Shea off, she decided to forgive him for leaving so early. He worked hard and deserved a bit of playtime to himself. Besides, she was looking forward to what he had in mind for *later*, especially if it was anything like the wicked, carnal things he'd done to her during the course of the night and early this morning.

Feeling lazy and relaxed, she took a long, hot shower and put on a tank top and a gauze skirt. Since Shea wouldn't be jogging this morning, Claire decided to take a walk on the beach, as she sometimes did. She headed down to the water's edge and strolled along the stretch of beach, her mind filled with thoughts of Shea.

After last night, there was no doubt in her mind that she was falling hard and fast for him. They'd only gone out a few times, but she'd shared more with him than she'd ever intended, mainly because he'd been so easy to talk to. She'd trusted him with the humiliating details of her divorce, and she'd let him see her vulnerable, insecure side. It had felt so incredibly good to have such a strong connection with Shea that she could share anything with him, especially since it had been a long time—if ever—since a man had been so interested in everything about *her*.

An hour later, she returned to her house, ready to get to work and finish the ring she'd started last night. Pouring herself a cup of coffee, she carried it into the living room, settled herself on the chair in front of her drafting table, and picked up the gold setting she'd worked on yesterday. She checked the prongs on the diamonds, tightened them in a few places, and knew she was ready to add the crowning glory to the design—the Padparadsha sapphire.

She started to slide off her seat to go and get the gem from her safe, then remembered that she'd had it out when Shea had arrived last night. She'd been so distracted and so eager to be with him that she'd forgotten to lock it up again.

Reaching for the velvet pouch where she kept the stone, she opened the small bag, but there was no jewel inside. Startled by the realization, she checked the surface of the table, including picking up her jeweler's tools and shuffling through her designs just in case the gem was hiding somewhere. When that didn't produce what she was looking for, she got on her hands and knees and checked the floor around where she worked—with the help of Zoey, who was curious to know what she was doing.

Feeling desperate and panicked, she dumped out the small trash can she kept beside the drafting table and rifled through the crumpled papers and other debris. When that didn't produce the stone either, she rechecked everything all over again, hoping that she'd somehow missed the gem.

The sapphire was nowhere to be found.

A sickening, dreadful sensation swirled in the pit of her belly as she realized that she'd left the living room sliding door unlocked when she'd gone out for her walk on the beach. It had always been easier to leave the door open than to carry her keys with her, and she'd never experienced any problems. Now, with her rare and expensive sapphire gone, she was questioning the wisdom of her decision.

She also had to face the fact that someone had stolen the Padparadsha, and there was only one thing left for her to do.

She picked up the phone and called the police to file a theft report. Despite the fact that the stone was insured and she'd likely be reimbursed, the whole incident left her feeling violated. Needing to hear Shea's voice, she called him to tell him what had happened. He'd been concerned by the news, but also distracted by a delivery that arrived while they were on the phone, as well as supervising tile work being done behind the bar area, and promised to come by later.

A uniformed officer arrived at Claire's within the hour and began the investigation process for her claim.

"There don't seem to be any signs of a break-in," the cop, who went by the name of Garrett, said. "So, most likely the perpetrator came in through the sliding glass door from the deck."

Claire wrapped her arms around her churning stomach. Even though she had suspected as much, she hated hearing the truth out loud. Knowing that someone had been inside her house without her knowledge and had possibly gone through her things was a huge shock. While she'd only noticed that the sapphire was missing, she couldn't help but wonder if they'd taken anything else of value that she wasn't aware of yet.

"Has anyone had any access to the inside of the house lately?" the officer asked as he glanced up from his note-pad. "A housekeeper? A maintenance person, possibly?"

She shook her head. "No."

"How about any friends over the past few days?"

Shea was more than a friend, but she wasn't about to clarify that Shea was her lover to the policeman. "Well, yes, but he doesn't have anything to do with this."

"I understand, but I'd like to get the person's name, any-way," he replied patiently. "It's standard procedure for this kind of investigation."

She hesitated, then gave the man the information he was after. "There's only one person who has been in the house since I moved in a few weeks ago. His name is Shea O'Brien."

After jotting down the name on his notepad, Garrett glanced up at her, his gaze direct. "Does he know about this valuable stone you have?"

The man's stare made her feel uneasy, and she fought the instinctive urge to defend Shea. "Yes, he does."

"I think that's about it." The officer snapped his book shut and tucked his pen into his shirt pocket, then retrieved a business card and handed it to her. "I'll get a report typed up for you so you can use it for your insurance claim. Call me if anything pertinent comes to mind, and if I find out anything else during the investigative process, I'll be sure to let you know."

"Thank you," she said, and walked him to the door. "I appreciate it."

The officer left, and Claire was surprised to get a phone call from him later that afternoon. She was even more stunned to hear what he had to say.

"Ms. Reissing, I had one of the detectives here at the station run a background check on your friend, Shea O'Brien," he said, concern in his tone. "Did you know that he has a prior criminal record?"

Her entire body went cold, and she prayed that she'd misheard him. "Excuse me?"

"He's been previously arrested for stealing a valuable gemstone from a collector," he said, and this time Claire heard him clearly. "Were you aware of this?"

The officer's incriminating words rang in her ears, and she had to sit down on the couch because her legs had gone weak and she felt physically ill. *Shea was a jewel thief.*

Zoey came up to her and rubbed against her legs, as if sensing something was wrong, and Claire found comfort in the cat's affectionate gesture. Especially when everything else around her seemed to be falling apart.

"I had no idea," she finally said, her voice a rasp of sound.

"Would you like me to have the detective call him in for questioning?"

She squeezed her eyes shut, wishing this was all a bad dream, except when she opened her eyes again, she was very wide awake and she had a difficult choice to make. Either send Shea to the police station to find out what he knew about her missing gemstone, or confront him herself.

It wasn't an easy decision, but after everything they'd shared—or rather, everything *she'd* shared with *him*—there was only one option for her.

"No, I'd like to talk to him myself," she said. She deserved to hear the truth straight from the man who'd deceived her.

"All right," the officer replied. "But if you change your mind, give me a call."

They hung up, and a combination of hurt and anger swelled within her when she thought back to the day Shea had saved her from that current. Obviously, something like that couldn't have been planned, but she had shown him the Padparadsha that morning. She remembered his interest, and his knowledge of gemstones, and how Shea had claimed his father was a collector. It had been a logical explanation, and believing him had been so easy.

She felt duped and used, and this betrayal cut to the core of who she was because of how deeply she'd fallen for Shea, and how fast. Everything between them had been a lie, a calculated ploy for him to get closer to her, which in turn put him in the prime position to steal the sapphire and escape suspicion.

Her throat clogged with emotion and self-recriminations. She was much too trusting, and now she was twice a fool. First with Alan, and again with Shea. It was as though her recent past was repeating itself, and she had no one to blame for her naivete but herself, for letting yet another man sweep her off her feet and blind her to his faults.

She wanted her Padparadsha back, and then she was swearing off men for a good long time.

* * *

It was after eleven at night when Shea arrived at Claire's, and as soon as he walked into her place he knew something was very wrong. The chill in her stance was palpable, and every time he stepped near her she'd back away, deliberately avoiding any kind of contact with him.

He tried to push away the increasing unease creeping over him, but failed. "I'm really sorry I'm late," he apologized as he followed her into the living room. "I had to fill in for Mark since he was out and it was busier than usual. What happened with the police today?"

She stopped by the couch and turned around to face him, her gaze lacking any of the warmth he normally saw in her eyes. "They were very helpful, actually."

Since she didn't sit down, neither did he, and the tension within him grew. "Any clues as to who might have broken in?"

"According to them, no one broke in. They most likely came and left through the unlocked sliding glass door." Her chin lifted in a defensive gesture. "Why didn't you tell me you were a jewel thief?"

Her question hit him like a punch in the chest—a hard and unexpected blow that left him momentarily speechless. "I'm not a jewel thief," he said succinctly.

Disbelief transformed her expression. "So, you've never stolen a gem from a collector before?"

Admitting the truth would alienate her more, Shea knew, but he didn't even consider lying. "Yes, I did. Once. A long time ago."

"And you didn't think telling me the fact that you were arrested for theft was important?"

The hurt in her voice was unmistakable, and he hated that he was the cause of her pain. He attempted to explain, to give her the answers that would make her understand. "Claire, I didn't—"

"Think it would matter?" she said before he could finish his sentence. She was too upset, too angry to listen to him. "Or maybe you didn't want me to know the truth about you so it would make it easier for you to get close to me and steal the sapphire?"

The accusation sliced in the air between them, sharp as a knife, and cutting just as deep. "Is that what you honestly believe?"

"What else can I believe?"

"That I care about you," he said, putting his feelings for her out in the open in hopes that it would make some kind of difference. "That I'd never hurt you, let alone use you to steal something that was yours."

She crossed her arms over her chest, and for a moment Shea thought she was going to soften and give him the benefit of the doubt. Then, as he watched, her features grew cool and guarded once again. "I'd like the Padparadsha back," she said, her tone emotionless.

Frustrated, he jammed his hands onto his hips. "I didn't take it."

She sighed, the sound rife with sadness. "Shea, I don't want to get the police involved, but I will if I have to."

Unable to break through her walls, his own anger finally got the best of him. "Then you do what you have to do, Claire, because they won't find a thing on me. I'm clean. And for the record, I didn't tell you about my past because I was afraid you'd never give me a chance. And it's true, isn't it?"

She didn't reply, which was an answer in itself.

He went on. "Then, when you told me about what Alan had done to you, I knew you'd run far and fast if you knew the truth about me and my past."

"Well, it doesn't matter now," she said quietly.

He hated being brushed off. Hated even more that she believed the worst of him. "Yeah, it does matter, because I'm not the thief that you think I am."

She laughed, but the sound lacked any real humor. "But you were convicted of stealing a valuable jewel from someone. That's kind of contradictory, don't you think?"

He clenched his teeth so hard his jaw ached. "Then let me explain."

She shook her head and took a step back, effectively putting physical and emotional distance between them. "It won't change anything."

A long, brittle silence filled the room, and Shea knew that there was little he could do to change Claire's mind. She was too wary because of Alan's lies and deceit, and she was protecting her heart and emotions the best she could. In a way he understood her caution, but she also had to believe in him, trust in him, if they had any chance at a future together. And that was something he couldn't force her to do, which meant this was possibly the end for them.

"Fine," he said, resigned. Since they were obviously done, he headed to the door, but stopped and turned before leaving. He met her gaze, and made sure she saw the sincerity in his. "Despite the mistakes I've made in my life, I'm not like your ex-husband, no matter what you think. When and if you're ever ready to hear my side of the story, and give me a chance to explain about my past, you know where to find me."

Then, knowing any chance with Claire was entirely up to her, he walked out of her house without looking back.

Claire crumpled up yet another sketch of a bracelet design that wasn't transferring to paper the way she'd imagined it in her mind. With an irritated sigh, she tossed the mashed paper toward the trash can and missed, adding to the other ones that littered the hardwood floor around her desk. Zoey pounced on the new toy and began batting it across the room, playing with the ball of paper with her usual enthusiasm.

Ever since she'd let Shea walk away three days ago, her inspiration had left right along with him. In its place was a huge ache in her heart, and a wealth of doubts and confusion about not giving Shea a chance to explain his past and his criminal record.

Now that she'd had plenty of time to think about everything, she regretted her hasty decision to pin him with the blame and wished that she hadn't jumped to conclusions. But having learned the news of Shea's past indiscretion from someone other than Shea himself, she'd been too hurt and angry to listen to reason, much less anything he had to say.

She'd told Shea that she was going to get the police involved in investigating him, but she hadn't been able to bring herself to call the detective handling the case to request that he bring Shea in for questioning. Her reluctance had to mean something, and most likely came from a deeper source—like the feminine instincts that were telling her that Shea was innocent and had nothing to do with the missing stone, no matter what he might have done in his past.

It was a huge leap of faith, but one she was ready to make—if Shea was even willing to see or talk to her again. There was always the possibility that he didn't want to have anything to do with her, considering the way she'd treated him.

His reason for not divulging his secrets to her so early in their relationship was understandable, and he'd been right to believe that she would have thought twice about getting involved with him if she knew the truth about his past. But looking back, she could honestly say that he'd shown her nothing but caring, support, and passion. And she wanted to believe with all her heart that Shea's interest in her had been real. In fact, she *did* believe it, which was why she was struggling with the urge to go and talk with him.

No one was perfect, and everyone made wrong choices in their lives. Hadn't she made her fair share? Granted, her lack of judgment hadn't landed her in jail, but she lived with regrets just like everyone else—and had hopefully learned from her mistakes.

It was only fair that she give Shea a chance to explain

his past. And in order to do that, she had to trust in her gut instinct that was telling her to believe Shea and the person he was.

She was ready to take that step with him.

Her decision made, she slid off the chair in front of her drafting table. It was after ten at night, and she hoped he'd be home from the pub for the evening. She needed to change, and that would give her time to get her thoughts together and figure out what to say to him.

As she started down the hall to her bedroom, she heard the sound of something tumbling lightly across the hard-wood floor—with Zoey chasing after it. Curious to know what the feisty cat was playing with, she went to check out what Zoey had found. The feline pounced on the object, then swatted it with her paw, sending the small item skittering toward Claire's bare feet.

She looked down and felt her stomach bottom out.

The light in the living room reflected off the brilliant gemstone she'd thought had been stolen. And it *had* been heisted . . . by her own cat. Zoey most likely had found the gem on Claire's drafting table the night Shea had come over, and had seen it as a playful object to bat around.

Claire picked up the jewel, not knowing whether to laugh at the irony of the situation, or cry at how much heartache the missing stone had caused her, and possibly Shea.

She had no idea if he'd forgive her for doubting him, but no matter the outcome, she owed him a huge apology.

CHAPTER ◆ SEVEN

The moment Shea opened the door to his house and his eyes widened in surprise, Claire knew that she was the last person he'd expected to see on his front porch. She wasn't sure whether to take that as a good sign or a bad one, but there was no turning back now, so she forged ahead.

"Hi," she said, offering a tentative smile. "Can I come in? I'd like to talk to you."

He hesitated for a heartbeat, just long enough to make her think he was going to refuse, before he finally answered. "Sure."

He opened the door wide, and she walked into the house, following him into his living room. Goldie came up to her and nudged her hand, and Claire gave the sweet dog a loving pat on the head before returning her attention to Shea, who was standing across the room from her. Just as she'd stood across the room from him a few days ago when she'd confronted him. Their roles had changed, giving her an idea of how Shea had felt when she'd put him on the spot the last time she'd seen him.

He looked the same as he had that night—gorgeous and sexy as always, but cautious and distant, even. Not that she could blame him for putting up his defenses when it came to her, especially after she'd accused him of a crime he hadn't committed. But that was *her* regret to bear, and she was here now to make amends. If he allowed her to.

"What's on your mind, Claire?" He sounded very businesslike, and not at all like the warm and caring Shea she knew.

"I've done a lot of thinking over the past few days, and I was wrong not to give you a chance to explain about your past." Her throat had gone dry from nerves, and she swallowed to moisten her mouth. "You told me that when I was ready to hear the truth that I knew where to find you. That's why I'm here. I'm ready now, Shea."

He tipped his head, studying her through narrowed eyes. "What changed your mind?"

Her fingers curled around the Padparadsha she'd put into the front pocket of her capris, but she'd decided not to tell him she'd found the stone just yet. She didn't want him to think that was the only reason why she was here now, giving him the chance to explain about his past. Regardless of whether the stone had appeared or not, she'd made the decision to have this conversation with him *before* Zoey had made the gem's whereabouts known.

"I have to admit that I was very upset when I found out

about your past from someone other than you. But you're right that I would have kept my distance if you'd come straight out and told me that you had a criminal record, so I do understand why you waited."

He crossed his arms over his wide chest and waited for her to continue.

"But once you were gone, something kept telling me that you were being honest with me and you had nothing to do with the sapphire's disappearance. Call it woman's intuition, or whatever you want, but it's enough for me to believe in you." She shifted on her feet, unsure whether her admission was enough to gain his forgiveness, but she wasn't giving up just yet. "Will you tell me about your past and what happened?"

With an unraveling sigh, he sat down on the couch and scrubbed a hand along his stubbled jaw. "It's not a pretty story."

"I don't care." And she didn't. All that mattered to her was his openness and honesty.

"All right. When I told you that my father collected rare and exotic gemstones, the truth is he acquired those expensive jewels by stealing them from collectors all over the world. He loved the thrill of eluding all types of security, and capturing the elusive."

"He was never caught?" she asked incredulously, and sat on the sofa across from him.

"Not once," Shea said with a shake of his head. "He was good at what he did, and while the police always suspected he was a jewel thief, there was never any evidence or proof to convict him."

Shea clasped his hands between his widespread knees and stared at the space between his feet. "Growing up, I was always trying to live up to my father's expectations, but I never seemed to please him. So, when I was twenty-one and cockier than I had any right to be, I set out to score a heist that would finally gain me my old man's admiration and respect. I knew he was after a rare twenty-three-carat yellow diamond that was recently acquired by someone my father knew, and I wanted to get it before he did."

He glanced back up at Claire, a wry smile on his lips. "I actually succeeded in lifting the stone before my father did, and sure enough, my old man was plenty impressed. But even though it felt good to have finally gained my father's approval, I never intended to keep the diamond. I had every intention of putting it back as quietly as I'd taken it, since the collector hadn't even realized it was gone."

Claire had a good idea where all this was heading. "But *you* got caught."

He nodded. "Only because the woman I was seeing at the time wanted me to keep the diamond for her, and when I told her I was returning it, she got angry and went to the police and told them what I'd done before I had the chance to put it back. The next thing I knew, I was in jail and convicted of grand theft."

She sucked in a breath. So, Shea had dealt with his own form of betrayal. True, he'd been wrong to steal the diamond in the first place, but to have the woman he cared about turn him in must have been devastating.

"Luckily, since I didn't have a prior record, and I returned the stolen jewel, I did very little time," he went on.

"But that experience was enough for me to swear off any idea I might have had about making it a career as my father did. Despite my old man's disappointment, I've been clean ever since," he said pointedly.

She knew exactly what he was insinuating—that he had no connection to the sapphire that had gone missing. "I know, and I owe you an apology," she said.

He frowned, confusion and uncertainty clouding his gaze. "For what?"

"For believing the worst. For not trusting in you." Standing, she retrieved the Padparadsha from her pocket, walked closer to him, and opened her hand so he could see the glittering gemstone nestled in her palm. "I'm truly sorry I ever doubted you or your intentions, Shea."

He glanced at the jewel, and then back up to her face, his caution reappearing again. "Are you saying that just because you found the sapphire and now know for certain that I had nothing to do with its disappearance?"

His entire body had gone tense, but she sat next to him on the sofa anyway, refusing to let him withdraw now that they'd come so far. "I know that's how it appears, but I came to the decision to trust in you *before* I found the sapphire. Or rather, before Zoey made its whereabouts known."

"Zoey?" he repeated in disbelief.

"Yeah, Zoey's the culprit," she said, unable to keep the amusement out of her voice. "She must have found it on my drafting table and knocked it to the floor when she was playing with it. I found her batting it around right before coming over here." She bit her bottom lip, then asked the most important question of the night. "Can you ever forgive me for believing the worst?"

"Only if you can forgive me for not being honest with you up front about my past."

Placing her hand on his cheek, she rested her forehead against his. "I already have. I don't care what happened years ago. All that matters to me is the man you are now. And since we're being so open with one another, I have to confess that I'm falling hard for you, Shea O'Brien."

"Thank God," he breathed, the sound filled with an abundance of relief.

She laughed, feeling lighthearted and incredibly happy. "I take it that's a good thing?"

"Very good, because I fell for you a long time ago and I've been waiting for what feels like forever for you to catch up to me." He grinned, and that was all it took to ignite the attraction between them.

"I think I'm already there," she said, and proved her feelings for him by giving in to the strong desire to kiss him, push him down on the sofa, and have her wicked way with him.

PARADISE BOSSED

MaryJanice Davidson

For Daniel and Lisa, who introduced us to the real paradise that is Little Cayman.

Also, thanks to the Cannon Falls Bombers, and all those pep rallies back in high school, which have made the Cannon fight song stick into my brain like a fishhook.

AUTHOR'S NOTE

The events of this story take place about a year and a half after the events in "The Fixer-Upper" (*Men at Work,* Berkley Sensation anthology, December 2004). Also, snorkeling is usually a harmless activity.

"Cannon, Cannon, loyal are we.
Red and black we'll shoot you to victory.
So fight fight fight our motto will be.
Rah-rah-rah and sis-boom-bah!
Fight fight fight fight!
Go for the red and black!"
—Cannon Falls High School Fight Song

"You'd bitch if they hung you with a new rope."
—Alexander Davidson III

"I see dead people."
    "In your dreams . . . while you're awake? Dead people like
in graves? In coffins?"
    "Walking around like regular people. They don't see each
other. They only see what they want to see. They don't know
they're dead."
—From *The Sixth Sense*

◆ PROLOGUE

St. Paul, Minnesota
February 21, 1975

Jack watched with interest as his sister's nosy-body neighbor dragged a GP (General Psychic) into his house.

It was actually his sister's house; it had passed to her on their parents' deaths. But they both knew whose house it really was. Jack had lived there for many years. His sister was getting on, but he felt just the same.

"You can't mean to *live* like this," Nosy-body was saying. "Who lives like this?"

"Well." His sister looked around helplessly, but Jack decided not to come to her assistance, this once. She really did need to learn how to stand up for herself. It was his fault she couldn't, and now it was too late. Forty years too late.

But if an old dog like him could learn, maybe she could, too. "Well, we get along fine, Jack and me."

"No, no. You must get him out. You can't have a—a dead thing running amok in your own house. It's—outrageous! Your chakra and your aura are completely screwed up." Nosy-body rattled the purple beads around her neck as if to make a point. She was wearing a black T-shirt that had a pair of giant red lips on the front. She was an infant at twenty-seven.

"Well, it would have been Jack's house if he hadn't broken his neck in the basement," his sister said reasonably, and Jack almost groaned. "Really, I think of it as his house."

The medium, who hadn't said a word to that point, was looking around at the carefully kept Victorian with an almost bored look on his face. He was holding hands with a small, curly-haired blond boy, a boy with the bluest eyes and dirtiest green coat Jack had ever seen. The child looked like an angel down on his luck.

"You'll never get the damned thing out," the angel said.

"Think so, Tommy?" The medium, who had the same curly hair (less vivid than the boy's), dirty clothes, and blue eyes, seemed unsurprised at the child's tone and language.

"Dad, you can't do it. Nobody could do it." The child paused, his eyes narrowing with thought. "Maybe Mr. Graham in London. Nobody here."

"Sorry, then, ladies," the medium said.

"But you haven't even taken your coats—"

"If Tommy—"

"Tom," the child corrected, bored.

"If my son says it's a no-go, it's a no-go. He's much stronger than me, you see." The medium offered a small smile, which didn't match his eyes.

"Besides, he's not hurting anybody," the child added, apparently in response to the stunned look on the faces of the two ladies. "He helps you, doesn't he, Miss Carroll?"

"Well, yes, I don't know how I'd get along without my Jacky. . . ."

"Yeah, well, that's the problem," the child said. "S'long as you both feel so strongly about helping each other out, he'll never leave. And nobody will ever get him out."

"Er . . . oh."

"Good-bye," the child said, almost politely.

"Good-bye, dear. Thank you—thank you both—for coming."

"Bye, Jack."

Jack knocked once in response, making Nosy-body jump. The child didn't even turn, and the father was half-way out the door already.

That poor boy! He was, what? Four? Five? And how much of the human condition had he already seen? Murder, sex, greed, thievery, vanity—it made Jack shiver to think about it.

"Not one of my finer moments," his sister said when they had left.

He knocked.

"I know, I know, I should have told Sharon I wasn't interested. Because I wasn't, you know. She just has a way of—taking over, I guess. All that chakra talk makes a lady tired." She paused, waiting, and then added, "And I'd never get rid of you, darling."

Sulking, Jack didn't respond.

"But I must admit I was curious."

Jack restrained himself from snorting.

"And I also have to admit I wanted to meet a famous medium." While she chattered, she set the pot on for tea and rummaged through the cupboards. She was a tea snob, and would no sooner use a Lipton bag than go outside without a girdle.

"Thomas Fillman is supposed to be the most powerful psychic in the Midwest. But I see it's Thomas Jr. who's the real talent. That poor baby! Better at five than his father ever was, and now he's being dragged all over town to dig through old houses, looking for ghosts. . . . I could cry right now."

Well, don't, Jack thought. *It's none of our business.*

Still, he couldn't help wondering, as the years passed, how the child was doing, and if he was happy.

CHAPTER ◆ ONE

Little Cayman, 2006

Nikki floated through the azure waters beyond Little Cayman like a—well, like an angel, thank you very much! Her long blond hair was fanning out behind her as she twirled and whirled through the water, dancing like a water sprite, wriggling through schools of fish like . . . like . . .

Like someone who's got to get a grip, she thought, and snorted, and then had to swim to the surface.

She spit out the mouthpiece, along with a mouthful of seawater. "Angel!" she crowed, and only the gulls heard her. They spun overhead, laughing at her. Natch! Angel. Shit.

She dipped her head back in the water, skimming the long strands away from her face (ah, they were like strands of kelpy, smelly seaweed, that was romantic, right?), then adjusted her mask and bit into the big rubber nipple.

Then she dove back down to examine the glory that was Little Cayman Island. She should have gone back and re-slathered sunscreen, but dammit, she was having too much fun.

And soon enough, she'd be out here constantly; Pirate's Point Resort wasn't that big—maybe ten guests, total, and most of them on the boat all day. Cathy and Jack, who didn't dive, would be necking all over the place. Nikki felt like enough of a third wheel at home; she had no intention of feeling like that on her vacation.

It wasn't their fault, and they weren't doing anything wrong. Cathy was newly in love, ditto Jack, and after eighty zillion years, Jack was starved for sex, touching, hugging, kissing, even handshakes. A trip to the store to get milk could quickly end up an X-rated straight-to-video incident.

She was nuts to have accepted their invitation—it was their anniversary, for God's sake.

That said, she'd also have been nuts to turn down a free trip to the Cayman Islands . . . although why Cathy had a jones on about coming to a place famous for scuba diving, when neither of them dived, was a mystery. It was like deciding to go to Antarctica when you didn't like penguins, or the cold.

She swam down, wiggling her flippers to get as close as possible to the sea floor. Schools and schools of fish swam by, ignoring her—to them she was just another skinny tourist in a Target bikini. But Christ! It was like being on the Discovery Channel. Fish and coral—live coral, no less—and birds above and turtles below. Unreal. Here she'd been going to Disney World every year, with no idea what she was missing.

She saw something out of the corner of her eye and turned to get a better look, then jerked back, startled. Stingray. Nice-sized, too—a six-foot wingspan. It wouldn't hurt her; rays were huge but gentle, and this one was startled, and as it flinched away from her, the barbed tail whacked her, quite by accident, across the side of her face.

But that was okay, because they were harmless, you just had to watch out for the—for the thing—the thing on the end of their—

Luckily, her face didn't hurt. And the blood in the water—it probably wasn't hers. And even if it did attract sharks, there was nothing in these waters that could hurt her. Not even rays—they only stung you if you stepped on them by accident. That's what her instructor told her, and he knew his shit. Besides, it hadn't even hurt.

No, nothing hurt; everything was numb. She'd figured on swimming up for another breath of air, but she didn't need one now.

She brought a hand up to touch her face and missed. Were her lips gone? Or was she too numb to find them? She swam to get to the surface, and bumped into the ocean floor.

This is not good, she told herself, but really, it was impossible to get worked up over it. It was so beautiful here, so peaceful. She was almost a part of it, lying on the floor in the rich silt, a part of the fish and even the saucy ray who had smacked her by accident and gone on its way.

She pulled off her mask and snorkel. Ah! That was better. Now she could breathe. It was a lot harder, breathing water than air, but she was up to the challenge.

It was too bad, though. She herself didn't mind so much, but her pal Cathy would completely lose it when she heard the news.

CHAPTER ◆ TWO

"What do you mean, 'missing and presumed'?" Cathy shrieked. "What does that mean? Why aren't we looking for her? Why weren't you looking earlier?"

"Is she dead?" Jack asked. "I guess you'd better tell us if she's dead."

"Of course she's not dead, she's just snorkeling. Right?"

"For eighteen hours?" her husband asked gently.

Cathy clawed through her hair, the curly dark hair Nikki so admired. And still did admire! Not past tense: present tense. Nikki was very much in the pesent tense, nothing was wrong, it was all a stupid misunderstanding, that was all, just a—

". . . came alone, and we're pretty casual here. . . . You can keep the snorkeling gear in your room and go out whenever you want. We have no idea when she left, but she wasn't at supper last night, or breakfast this morning, so we alerted the coast guard as well as—"

"Nobody's seen her since last night? Well, we—we—" She cast around. "We have to find her, then. That's all. We just have to. She's a good swimmer but she's not used to the ocean—we live in Minnesota—and she'll be waiting for us to get her . . ." Cathy burst into tears, and was instantly pissed at herself for doing it. This accomplished nothing. It slowed everything down.

Her husband, cool as a flounder in most situations, patted her but fixed his gaze on the guide, waiting patiently for an answer to his question.

"Yes," the guide said with great reluctance. "I think she's dead."

"Of course she is, she's been dead since last night, only she was alone and no one noticed. She was *alone*," Cathy said, and did something she had never done before, and hoped never to do again: she fainted.

She woke up in their room, their little cabana on the ocean. Jack looked calm and unconcerned, but then, he always did. He *looked* like a twentysomething handyman who had to struggle with *Body Art Monthly*, when in fact he was a hundred-year-old intellectual.

"They're still looking," he said, patting her wrist. She saw he'd taken off her shoes and placed her neatly in the middle of the bed. "They'll find her."

"That's what I'm afraid of," she said, and rolled over to

bury her face in the pillow. "I'll never forgive myself, never!"

"Honey, I didn't catch that."

She rolled back over. "I said I'll never forgive myself. She came down here *alone* and we were all supposed to be together, only she came down *alone*, and we should have noticed when she didn't come back from snorkeling, we *should* have! Who dies going *snorkeling*, for God's sake?"

"Well," Jack began cautiously, then stopped. It was just as well; what could he have said? He had died falling down the basement stairs. Talk about senseless.

"What if they never find her?" she asked. "What if she gets . . . you know. Eaten."

Jack just shook his head, and she suppressed a flare of temper. Most men would be all "There, there." Jack knew too much, had seen too much. He wouldn't comfort her if he thought it was a lie.

"Well, we're not going anywhere until we find her. Hear that?"

"I hear that," he replied.

"Thank God I quit my job last month," she muttered, throwing a forearm over her eyes.

"I have money," he reminded her.

A bundle. His sister, a lovely woman still living in a St. Paul nursing home, had figured out their secret, and insisted on giving half her inheritance to Jack. Or, rather, the body Jack now lived in. It had amounted to several million dollars, and had certainly taken the pressure off.

No more temp jobs for her, and plenty of money for new carpeting.

The thought of her happiness, of the *money* making her *happy*, when now her best friend was most likely shark supper, made her burst into fresh tears.

CHAPTER ◆ THREE

Oh this is so BOGUS.

And not a little bogus, either. Big, gooey, lame bogus. Unendurably bogus.

I hated the movie Ghost. *Demi Moore dripping tears over everything that moved, stupid Patrick Swayze getting his damn self shot, stupid Whoopi Goldberg—well, she wasn't so bad . . .*

Nikki knocked on the cabin door, forgetting, again, that she was incorporeal. The ghost thing was tough to get used to. Worse than passing bio in college!

Her fist passed through the wood of the door and she hesitated. She'd been through three other cabins, looking for Jack and Cathy. This could be lucky number four. That was good, right? Right. Only, she prayed they weren't doing it.

She stuck her head through the door. Success! There

they were, Cathy sobbing (nuts) on the bed as if, uh, she'd lost her best friend (okay, she had), and Jack sitting beside the bed, his chin resting on one fist, watching her with a glum look. He was shirtless, in khaki shorts, deeply tanned, and even in the middle of her rather large problem, she noticed for the hundredth time how yummy her best friend's husband was.

Who was tan in March? They lived in Minnesota, for goodness sake.

"Sorry to ogle," she said cheerfully, "but it's your own fault for letting him walk around without a shirt."

Nothing.

"Guys! I'm okay! Well, relatively speaking."

"I'll never forgive myself," Cathy said, her voice thick with tears.

"You did nothing wrong, love." Jack's voice was a soothing rumble.

"I just can't stand the thought of her floating around out there, all alone—Nikki hates being by herself."

"Uh, guys?"

"Cathy, you've got to stop. You've been crying for hours. You'll make yourself ill."

"Guys?" She walked over to them—she might be able to pass through walls, but an old habit like walking on the floor was hard to break—and waved her hands in front of them. "Guys? I'm here. I'm okay. Relativ—never mind. Don't cry, honey, you know how your nose swells up."

"I can't help it," Cathy cried. "This was supposed to be a fun vacation for the three of us, and now what? The coast guard is looking for my best friend's body."

"They are? Oh, great. I guess." She grimaced at the thought of gorgeous tropical fish nibbling on her toes. Had she sunk? Was she floating? The salt water was going to be murder on her hair. . . .

"Because of you," Cathy accused. "You just had to finish that damned painting."

"Don't go blaming him," Nikki said sharply. "It was a silly accident."

Jack's mouth tightened for a moment, then he replied, most gently, "Love, Nikki wouldn't want you carrying on like this."

"Yes I would! I mean, you guys can mourn for a day. That's all right."

"I can't help it," Cathy said again.

"You must. It's been a week. You have to try to calm down. You must think of the baby."

"The *baby*?" Nikki almost yelled.

"I'm sorry for what I said," Cathy said. "It was my fault, too. I wanted to stay for the doctor's appointment."

"Baby?" Nikki shouted again. "Oh, nice! You let him knock you up, and you were gonna tell me when? Jerks!"

Then it hit her: a week? But she'd only died a couple of hours ago! Sure, it had taken her a while to get back to the island and find their cabin, but—

"I guess you're right," Cathy sighed, sitting up. Jack got up at once and went to the bathroom. Nikki heard the sound of running water, and then he came back out holding a full glass. "Thanks."

"Drink it all," he told her. "You don't want to become dehydrated in this heat."

"Jerks! I'm in the room, you know. What, you're all done mourning now?" Although, the thought of Cathy crying nonstop for a week (a week?) was sort of dismaying. Especially if she was *el preggo.* "Can you really not see me?"

She stuck her arm through Jack's head. He didn't notice. Didn't even get a cold chill, like in the movies. And the guy had been a ghost himself for, like, eighty years.

She thought of *The Sixth Sense,* the most horrifying movie in the history of cinema. She had been mesmerized. That poor kid. Poor Bruce Willis.

But, what was worse than seeing dead people?

Not being seen at all.

"Jerks," she said again. It was lame, but it was all she could think of.

"Let's go back to the lodge, see if they found—if they found anything."

"You mean," Nikki said, "if they've stumbled across my rotting corpse."

Jack got up again. "You stay here and try to relax." He rested his hand on her annoyingly flat stomach, and Nikki thought, *The true, awful irony of death: I still have cellulite.* "I'll go check."

"Hurry back," Cathy practically begged.

"I will. Rest."

He walked through (yeesh!) Nikki, making her windmill her arms in surprise, opened the door, and was gone.

She rushed to the bed. "Cathy! Cath, it's me." She waved frantically as her friend sighed and gulped and sniveled. "Come on, we're—we were—best friends. There's a bond!

There was a bond. Argh. Fucking past tense. You've got to see me."

Cathy groped for a tissue and noisily blew her nose.

"See me!" Nikki yelled. "Dammit! People are scared shitless of ghosts! You're supposed to see my bad dead self and freak out!"

Cathy sighed and stared at the ceiling, tears leaking from her big blue eyes and puddling in her ears.

"Okay, remember this? I was too tall for cheerleading and you were too lame, but we learned the cheers anyway."

She threw her arms up in a V for victory.

Cannon, Cannon, loyal are we.
Red and black we'll shoot you to victory.
So fight fight fight our motto will be.
Rah-rah-rah and sis-boom-bah!
Fight fight fight fight!
Go for the red and black!

She leapt in the air, limbs akimbo. "Yaaaaaaayyyyy!"

Cathy cried harder. Not that Nikki could blame her.

"Dammit," she said, and plopped into the chair recently vacated by Jack. She had so much momentum she slipped through it, through the floor, and a good four feet into the ground, which really gave her something to swear about.

CHAPTER ◆ FOUR

She had prowled every inch of Little Cayman (or maybe *haunted* was the word) and except for the resort guests and the iguanas, there was nothing but sand and nauseatingly gorgeous beaches.

Nothing had changed. Cathy had been crying on and off, Jack had been stoic, the cook had produced magnificent meals, and the coast guard boats kept chugging up and down the beaches, sometimes very close to the dry sand (she was amazed the boats didn't beach themselves, like whales), sometimes little dots on the horizon.

Morbidly, Nikki wondered how much longer they'd search. And where the hell was her body, anyway? Probably in the gut of some damn great white.

She had tried talking, yelling, screeching, cheering, walking through them—nothing. Nobody else on the island could see her, either.

Was this it? No bright light? No afterlife? Just stuck watching her best friend's misery? Even Patrick Swayze got the bright light, after a while. This—this was unbearable. She had never dreamed being dead would be so bad, but watching your friends suffer was hell.

Due to the tragedy of her untimely death, she, Cathy, and Jack were the only guests at Pirate's Point. Everyone else couldn't get back to the small airport fast enough. Nobody wanted to go scuba diving, either—and who could blame them? Everyone was afraid of stumbling across her body.

The iguanas, usually fed fruit by indulgent guests, were getting bad off—certainly Cathy and Jack weren't in the mood to toss grapes at them. The boats stayed tied up; the snorkeling equipment stayed in the shed.

If this went on much longer, the tiny resort would really be hurting.

But Jack and Cathy wouldn't go home. Nikki had no idea how to feel about that. Relieved? Annoyed? If they left, she'd be by herself. But they couldn't keep hanging around Little Cayman until . . . until. That was just . . .

She walked through the south wall of cabin 3 just in time to see a naked Jack climb on top of her (naked) best friend. She had a horrifying glimpse of hairy ass and Cathy's pale flailing limbs before she gagged and lurched back out the wall. Not fast enough, unfortunately, to drown out Cathy's "Jack, Jack! Do it now!" and Jack's rumbly "Ah, my sweet fragrant darling . . ."

"Nice!" she hollered. "I'm dead and you two are boning—again! Or celebrating life. Whatever. Still, take a breather once in a while, willya? It's the middle of the day. Besides, how many times can you get her pregnant in a—a—month?"

How long had it been? Time, she had discovered in death, was a slippery concept. The sun raced across the sky, followed by the moon, and although it only felt like a couple of days, Cathy was already showing.

She decided, trudging back to the lodge, that as fine as Jack was, if she never saw his hairy crack again, she'd be happy forever.

Fragrant darling?

She put the thought out of her mind, quick.

CHAPTER ◆ FIVE

"I think we should call a medium."

It was chilly in the small hut—the wall unit was going full blast to combat the tropical heat outside—and Cathy pulled a blanket over her legs. "A medium what?"

"A psychic."

"To help us find the body." It wasn't a question. Jack had been on the spirit plane for almost a century; it was natural that he would think of such a thing. "Maybe—talk to Nikki?"

"Maybe. It's something, anyway. Better than waiting for . . . better than waiting."

She stroked his long thigh. "I guess it sounds like a silly complaint, but three months in paradise is too much. And it's no fun without Nikki here."

"Thanks," Jack said dryly.

"I'm sorry, babe. You know what I mean. Everything's, you know, unfinished. I feel like I'm in limbo."

Unseen by both, Nicki stuck her head through the wall and yelled, "*You* feel like you're in limbo?"

"Yes," Jack agreed as if he hadn't been interrupted. Which, in a way, he hadn't.

"Do you know who to call?"

Nikki popped back in. "Oh, we're in a rerun of *Ghostbusters* now? 'Who you gonna call? Nikki-busters!'"

"I mean," Cathy continued, "how do you find a psychic?"

"I know exactly who to call—not the medium, but the medium's intermediate. She can put us in touch. The boy would be"—Jack's dark eyes narrowed in thought—"well into his thirties. Assuming he's still in the business."

"One way to find out," Cathy said, and got up to get dressed.

Three days later

Nikki was gratified to see Jack and Cathy come out of their cabin after the sun had set. She didn't want to risk interrupting another (gag) intimate moment and besides, she had high hopes. It was a full moon (again) and if she knew her spooky movies and Ouija board fiction, it was a great time for spirits to speak to the living.

"Guys!" she said, following them to the lodge. Their footprints sank deep in the sand; she, Nikki observed glumly, left none. "It's still me. Still Nikki. Don't you think it's about time you noticed me? You know, if you can stop having sex for five minutes."

The lodge van, a tasteful serial-killer gray, pulled into the drive, and her friends hurried to meet it.

That was weird. There hadn't been any new guests since—well.

"Let's try a new one," she said, trailing after them like a puppy. "You've gotta remember this one, Cath. We worked on our walkovers for six months to get it right. Remember? We went to Michigan with my folks that time and memorized it? Cath? Remember?"

The van's engine cut off, and the driver and a lone passenger got out. Nikki, focused on her friends, ignored them.

She punched a fist through the air and cheered:

Let's give a cheer for dear old Traverse
Come on and boost that score sky high
And let the north woods ring with glory
For the tales of Central High.

She took another breath (force of habit), made a V for victory, clapped, and continued.

And watch out you who stand against us
For we're out to win tonight.
We're gonna add to the glory
Of the—

"God, will you stop making that noise?" the passenger said, clearly irritated. "I've already got a headache from all the plane rides."

"What?" Cathy said.

"What?" Nikki said.

CHAPTER ◆ SIX

He was a tall drink, at least six feet five, and thin—
too thin, like he forgot to eat regularly. He had a headful of
blond, shoulder-length waves—the moonlight bounced off
them in a romantic, yet weird way—and the palest, bluest
eyes Nikki had ever seen. Pilot eyes. Shooter's eyes. He
hadn't had a chance to shave in a couple of days, and the
beard coming in was surprisingly dark and coarse.

"Is this a joke? It must be. I fly two thousand miles to
listen to a dead cheerleader reliving her glory days."

"Hey!" Nikki snapped. "I was never a cheerleader. Too
tall." Then she realized what was happening. "Wait a damn
minute. You can hear me?"

"She didn't make cheerleading," Cathy was saying sor-
rowfully. "She was too tall. But we had fun practicing
together. That's amazing, that you would know that. Did
your psychic vibrations tell you that?"

"The only vibrations I get are when I lean up against the washing machine."

"In lieu of regular dating, I guess," Nikki snarked.

"Shut up, what do you know about it?"

"So how did you—Did you study up on her background before you came here?" Cathy was asking.

"Please," the man said, rolling his blue, blue eyes. Then he looked at Jack. "What are *you* doing alive again? That's not your body."

"It is now," Jack said. "It's nice to see you again, Tommy."

"Tom," the man corrected. "For God's sake. I'm too big to be a Tommy."

"This is my wife, Cathy, and—"

"Do you think you can find her?" Cathy interrupted.

"What's to find? She's here."

"Yippee! Finally, someone can hear me!"

"Yeah, lucky me," Tom said sourly.

She jumped up and down in her excitement and he flinched. "Don't. For the love of God, don't do another cheer."

"I wasn't going to." Then she realized what he had actually said. "You can *see* me, too?"

"Yeah. You need to comb your hair."

She nearly reeled from a combination of surprise, relief, and rage. "Hey, at least I'm not sporting three days of stubble, jerk!"

"You mean she's here?" Cathy gasped. Fortunately, the driver had taken Tommy's beat-up bag into cabin 5, and it was just the four of them. "Right here?"

"Yes, and she won't shut up."

"*You* shut up."

"Tell her we're sorry," she begged, "and tell her—"

"She can hear you," Tom said, looking bored. "You just can't hear her."

"Tell her she must move on," Jack said, obviously forgetting the rules.

"Get lost," Tom said to Nikki. "Go away. Scram."

"Oh, suck my fat one," she said crossly. "Who died and made you king?"

Tom grinned, which was startling. It changed his whole face, took years off. Made him look, she had to admit, almost attractive. "Apparently you did."

CHAPTER ◆ SEVEN

Tom had gone from pooped to horny to annoyed to intrigued, in twenty-five seconds.

And normally, nothing would have gotten him out of his hometown (Pontiac, Missouri) just when it started to get perfect out: not the wet, overwhelming heat of summer, not the brown mid-temps of winter. But he couldn't say no to that kind of money, no matter how nice he'd gotten the yard to look.

As usual, it took him a second to figure out who was dead. What was not usual at all was how instantly attracted he was to the ghost. And what wasn't to like? A tall blonde in khaki shorts and a white oxford shirt; pink sandals and toenails the same shade. He knew it was how she pictured herself, the mental image she carried around, as opposed to what she'd actually been wearing when she died. Another surprise: most people saw themselves as unattractive and badly dressed.

And nobody on the other side (that he'd seen, so far) worked on cheers; they were much more concerned with finding forgiveness, or happiness, as opposed to spelling out *S-P-I-R-I-T* with their arms.

Heh.

"Thank you so much for coming," the man who used to be dead was saying. Tom remembered Jack Carroll well: It was seeing him alive in a new body that was surprising. Jack had been dead for decades, devoted to his sister, and stuck in a beat-up Victorian in St. Paul. "As you can see, we have a rather large problem."

"Who are you calling large?" the ghost said crossly.

"Heh," Tom said aloud. It was downright alarming; he couldn't take his eyes off her. He had a dozen questions for Jack and didn't care; the ghost was a thousand times more interesting.

What a damn shame he'd been hired to get rid of her.

"So, what's the problem?" he asked her.

"You mean, besides my untimely demise?" she replied. "I mean, I know how self-absorbed you probably think I am—"

"You and every other ghost I've met."

"Not that you should make snap judgments, but don't you think I'm entitled? Just this once? I mean, I'm dead!"

"And you shouldn't be here," he reminded her, inwardly thinking, *Of all the luck.*

"Tell me!"

"Oh," he said.

"Tell her," Mrs. Carroll interrupted (not that she knew she was interrupting), "that we're so sorry, and we'll do whatever she wants. What does she want?"

Tom waited. The ghost (he groped for the name and found it: Nikki) waited. Jack and Cathy Carroll waited. Finally, Tom said, "Aren't you going to answer her?"

Nikki started. "Oh. Right. I guess I was waiting for you to say 'They want to know what you want,' and then I'd answer, and you'd tell them what I said, and then they'd answer, and . . . you know."

"You don't speak English anymore? You lost your hearing when you lost your head?"

"Okay, okay. Tell 'em I'm fine. You know. Relatively speaking."

"She's fine," he said.

"But boy, this is going to get old, quick."

Normally, yes. He almost literally had to bite his tongue to stop from saying, "Naw, not this time."

"Don't you want to go to your cabin and freshen up, or whatever?"

He had; he'd forgotten his urgent need for a piss and a shower the second he'd spotted her, but now the urges came rushing back. "Yeah," he said. *Oh, you're impressing the hell out of her!* "Yeah." "Naw." *Great!*

On the heels of that thought: *Why do you want to impress a stranger? A dead stranger?*

"Well, I can wait. I mean, it's been a couple of months. What's another hour?" She smiled, flashing perfect American teeth. "I bet you've talked to people who've waited a lot longer."

That was true. But normally he didn't mind in the least making the dead wait. God knew they didn't hesitate to impose on him. But somehow, it seemed particularly awful to keep this woman waiting. Seemed awful to picture her moping around in the sand, hermit crabs crawling through her feet and the wind blowing right through her, and nobody seeing her, nobody at all.

He bit his lip and said, "Thanks. But I can freshen up anytime. You—what do you need?"

She looked surprised. "I dunno. What anybody wants, I guess—to make their budget, to get good gas mileage."

"That doesn't help us."

"Nikki," Cathy was asking, "what happened?"

"An accident," she replied. "I'm getting kind of vague on the details. I guess it doesn't matter, right? Dead is dead."

"An accident," Tom told the Carrolls.

Mrs. Carroll was rubbing her little potbelly and looking anxious. "But is she—but you're okay now? I mean—nothing hurts?"

"Not a thing," Nikki assured her friend. The shorter woman was looking a foot and a half to the left, but Tom didn't have the heart to tell her.

"If this were a movie, I guess we'd start looking for her killer."

"No!" Nikki nearly shouted. "Don't worry about my killer. Stupid thing's probably a hundred miles away by now, anyway. Don't hurt it."

"Shark?" Tom asked, and was immediately sorry when Mrs. Carroll—Cathy—looked stricken.

"Stingray."

"Stingray?" he repeated, in spite of trying to spare the Carrolls' feelings. "How'd you manage that?"

For the first time, the dead woman laughed. "Chum, it was just being in the wrong place at the wrong time. And I'm not really prone to that sort of thing."

"Once was the charm."

"Yeah," she said, laughing again. "It was the dumbest thing. You wouldn't believe."

"Try me," he said.

"Maybe later," she replied. "You really need a shower."

CHAPTER ◆ EIGHT

Nikki sat awkwardly on the bed, listening to the shower. Not that she had to stay out in the small bedroom/living room/sitting area; she could have popped into Tom's bathroom anytime she wanted. But being dead hadn't made her ruder. Much.

It was oddly comforting, this ritual. Pretending there were important things to do like waiting for guests to clean up. But what else was there to do? She'd assumed he'd wave his hands over her and she'd *poof!* to heaven or whatever. But nothing had happened. He and Cathy and Jack had just stood around, looking at each other. They couldn't even talk, because only Tom could see her.

The shower shut off. She again resisted the urge to take advantage of her ghost powers and stick her head through the door to check out his ass.

It was just about the most difficult thing she'd ever done; it wasn't like she had a lot of other ways to get her kicks these days. Oh, and it'd be morally wrong.

Speaking of morals, she was trying to keep them in mind as he opened the door and came out, damp and clean and wearing a pair of cutoffs. He grinned when he saw her. "Thanks for waiting."

"What am I supposed to say to that?" she almost snapped, then was sorry, then was annoyed she was sorry. "It's not like I had a choice," she said instead.

The smile fell away. "Right. Sorry."

"Me, too. Being dead makes me grumpy," she joked.

They looked at each other. "I've, uh, this has never happened before."

She blinked, which was interesting. It had to be pure force of habit—what did she need to blink, sweat, pee for? Finally, something good about being dead: no more bathroom worries. " 'This'?"

"I don't—I mean, I show up, find out what the d— the spirit needs, the spirit goes away, I go away. I mean, this . . ." He looked around the cabin. "It's almost . . . social."

"Believe me, I'd leave if I could. I think I'm stuck here. Here, the island," she added, "not here, your cabin."

"But you're not," he said, going to his bag and rummaging in it. "You've created this—You're here only because you think you—because you need to be."

Because I think I need to be? She decided to let the dig at her sanity pass. She was sure he didn't know how annoying he came off. *Gee, we've got so much in common.* "I don't *need* to be in the Caymans," she pointed out. "It's just a really nice bonus, being stuck in paradise."

"Obviously, part of you does need to be here." Annoyingly, he paused. "So what do you need?"

"Peace on earth, goodwill toward men?"

"'We're the United States government. We don't do that,'" he quoted.

"Oh!" She nearly jumped through the floor. "Greatest! Movie! Ever!"

He laughed. "You're in love with Robert Redford?"

"No, Dan Aykroyd."

"I've probably seen that movie a hundred times," he commented, gesturing her to move over so he could lie down on the bed. She almost cried; it was so nice to have someone interact with her. Him being a *Sneakers* fan was gravy on the roast. "Two hundred."

"Great concept, great script, great actors," she agreed. "And funny! One of the funniest movies I've seen."

"It was pretty funny."

"'Pretty funny'? Why, what's the funniest movie you've ever seen?"

"The Sixth Sense."

"Oh, boy. You're not serious." She peered more closely at him. "You're serious."

"Totally serious. I get the giggles just thinking about it." And he did; he started to laugh. "Dead people walking around all gory! The shrink didn't know he was one of them! And—"

"Wait, wait. We'll pass over the completely awful scariness of that movie to address this new issue: isn't it basically your life story?"

The laughing cut off like he'd flipped a circuit breaker. "No."

Ah. "I heard Jack saying you were, like, this really powerful psychic. I assume your power didn't just pop into your head when you hit twenty-one, right? You must have been doing this sort of thing when you were a kid, right?"

His jaw had gone tight, but his voice was casual, almost joking. "My power?" he asked. "What am I, in a Marvel comic book?"

Do Not Enter. He might as well have written it on his forehead. She pretended she knew he wasn't joking. "Hon, in case you haven't noticed, our lives—so to speak in my case—are a great big comic book."

He sighed and stared at the ceiling. "Some kind of fiction book, anyway."

"Did they scare you?" she asked quietly. "Do we scare you?"

He knew what she meant and answered readily enough. "No, not ever. Not even when I was a kid. The dead—spirits—don't have any power. They can't hurt us. Me, I mean. If I thought they were being too bossy I'd just ignore them. Believe me, when you're the only person they can talk to, ignoring them gets results"—he snapped his fingers—"like that."

"Thanks for the tip. Why do you keep correcting yourself and calling us spirits?"

"I, uh, don't want to make you mad."

There was an awkward pause. She squashed the strong urge to laugh off a serious moment with a bad joke and said, "Tom, that's the nicest thing anyone's said to me since I died."

He smiled, looking down at his lap.

"Please don't do that," she added. "You're the only one who looks at me when we're talking. I never thought—never thought I'd miss simple human interaction so much." She ground her teeth so she wouldn't cry. "It's all so—stupid. If you make fun of me I'll sic a stingray on you."

He stared at her for a long moment, then shot up off the bed. She assumed the airplane food was disagreeing with him until he said, "Come on," as he strode (well, the cabin was so small he was at the door in a stride and a half) to the door.

"Jinkies, Fred, did you solve the mystery?" She carefully got up—this was no time to go caroming through a wall. "What are we doing? What?"

"Simple human interaction," he replied, and out the door he went.

CHAPTER ◆ NINE

"Why did we come out here for this?" Nikki asked. "And when did the sun come back up?"

"I need your friends to keep an eye on my body," he muttered, sitting down and pulling his legs into a lotus position. "I might fall over."

"You must be putting me on," Jack commented, watching Tom fold himself into a gangly knot. "It isn't possible."

"What?" Cathy asked. "What is he going to do?"

"Simple human interaction."

"Yeah, whatever fit he's decided to have, it's my fault," Nikki explained to her friends, which was silly because they couldn't hear her. "I overshared and now he's freaked out."

"Mmmmmmmmmmmm," Tom said, shutting his eyes.

"You picked a rotten time to go crazy. Again, not to be all self-involved, but I'm pretty sure this whole thing is still about me."

"Mmmmmmmmmmm." Tom was still mmm'ing.

"It is impossible," Jack said. "And I do not say that lightly." Still, he didn't sound like he thought it was impossible. He sounded fascinated, like he couldn't wait to see what Tom was going to do next.

Nikki squatted in front of Lotus-Tom just in time to see him stand up. And now there were two Toms: Lotus-Tom and Ghost-Tom.

"How about that?" he beamed, standing over his own cross-legged body. He held his arms out. "That's worth a kiss at least, right?"

She blinked hard, reminded herself she didn't need to do that anymore, and cautiously reached out for him. His fingers closed over hers, warm and strong.

"Oh, boy," she said weakly. "Nice trick." And gave him the kiss he'd earned.

CHAPTER ◆ TEN

They were walking hand in hand on the beach, a picture right from of an ad agency travel poster, except, of course, neither of them was really there.

Her lips were still tingling from the kiss. He'd seized her so hard she'd nearly bent backward, she'd flung her arms around his neck so hard he'd nearly choked, and they'd mashed their mouths together like teenagers who had the equipment, but not the finesse. It had been the greatest kiss of her life.

What a damn shame.

"So, what's this? I mean, your physical body is back on the beach, but you're here with me?"

"Yup." He seemed abnormally cheerful.

"So you have two powers."

"Yup."

"What's this other one called?"

"Spirit walking."

"I had a pair of those once," she commented. "Easy Spirit walking shoes."

He punched her shoulder lightly. "Hilarious."

She was delighting in everything; his hand in hers, the roar of the surf, the texture of his beard (she'd have beard burn after that kiss, and that was just fine), his scent. Being incorporeal wasn't so bad if you had someone to be incorporeal *with*, and although she knew a large part of her problem had been loneliness, the truth was, she had been lonely before her encounter with Señor Stingray.

She had cried on Cathy's wedding day, but hadn't some of them been tears of jealousy?

"When I was little," he was saying, "I used to go right out to the spirits. I didn't realize until years later that I didn't have to do that, I could see and hear them just fine without having to leave my body. Still, it was fun—a great way to sneak out of the house."

She laughed so hard, she almost fell through the beach. "I'll bet! Leave your body all tucked in under the covers, then . . . *whoosh!* Oh, your poor parents."

He smiled down at her and she was struck again by his extreme height: he had five inches on her at least, and she was not a short woman. And his thinness. Shirtless, his collarbones looked like dull knives.

"You know, you really need a milkshake. And the food here is great. We've got to fatten you up. I mean, doesn't this"—she pinched his incorporeal arm for emphasis—"take it out of you?"

He shrugged.

"Because if it didn't, you'd probably do it all the time, right? And I bet you don't. Do that all the time, I mean." *Oh, God, I said "do it."*

He shrugged again. "It doesn't matter. I wanted to—" He almost choked off the rest of the sentence.

"What?"

"I wanted to touch you," he said, sounding like someone was strangling him. "See if you felt as good as you looked."

She stuck her foot between his ankles and he went sprawling on the beach, and then she pounced on him like a puppy with a new chew toy. "Yeah?" she challenged. "Well, I don't think you can tell by just one lousy kiss."

"Lousy?"

"It was terrible." She rubbed her chin into his chest and ignored his giggles. "Definitely time for a do-over. Remember that? When we were kids, if something didn't go right, you'd get a do-over?"

He stopped laughing. "I was never a kid." Then he cupped the back of her head with one big hand, pulled her down, and kissed her—almost bruised her—and she kissed him back. They were rolling around in the sand like a couple of beached flounders, and she thought, *There's something wrong with him. He's . . . broken.*

When they finished, they were lying inside a tree. "That can't be good for any of us," she said, standing up and automatically starting to brush off the sand—then remembered sand didn't stick to her anymore. She could go to the beach anytime she liked and not get sand get everywhere! Hmm, advantage number two. "Don't you want to get back to your body? Aren't you tired?"

"After *that*? Hell, no." He adjusted the waist on his shorts and grimaced. "Tired is the last thing I feel."

I won't look, I won't look, I—who am I kidding? She stole a peek at his bulging crotch, then said, "Forget it, pal. I'm not that kind of ghost."

"Just checking," he grumbled, and slung an arm around her shoulders, and they trudged back to the lodge.

CHAPTER ◆ ELEVEN

"Uh . . . where'd everybody go? And where's your body?"

"Good damned question."

Lotus-Tom was gone. She could see the marks in the sand where he'd been sitting, and there were more marks—drag marks? Like there'd been a scuffle? And then—

"Footprints," she said, and pointed. "Going back to your cabin."

"Mmmm." She could see he was pissed. She didn't blame him. How embarrassing to lose track of your physical body! She could relate. "Lucky for us you used to be a Girl Scout."

"I *did* used to be a Girl Scout, smart guy. Nobody in my troop sold more cookies than I did. *Nobody.* God, what I wouldn't do for a Thin Mint right about now."

He grunted, unmoved by her cookie lust, then marched to his cabin and walked through the door.

Wow! Do I look like that, all cool and vanish-ey? She did the same thing, and, since the cabins were so small (but then, who came to Little Cayman to hang out in their cabin?), nearly walked through the bed as well.

Lotus-Tom had been put on the bed, his legs untangled. And someone—Cathy, probably—had tucked the covers up to his chin.

"For God's sake," Ghost-Tom said.

Jack, sitting beside the bed and rereading *Your Essential Life*, didn't look up. Of course he didn't. But it was nice that they'd posted a guard.

Ghost-Tom was climbing into Lotus-Tom, who immediately sat up on the bed and said, "Don't ever do that again."

Jack dropped the book. "Don't ever do *that* again. I'm an old man; my heart can't take it."

"Spare me." Lotus-Tom—er, just Tom, now, she supposed, threw the covers back and climbed out of the bed. "I know you meant well, but it's really, really disturbing to come back to where you left your body and then have to look for it, all right?"

"Aw, get over yourself, ya big baby," Nikki commented helpfully, grinning when he shot her a glare.

"My wife was worried about you. She wanted to get you indoors, as there was no telling when you'd return to your—when you'd come back. So we brought you back here. Not without difficulty, I might add. You're a lot heavier than you look."

"Ohhh, snap," Nikki said.

"I have big bones," Tom said sulkily.

"My wife is resting, but I'll go wake her if you found anything out."

"Found anything out?"

"About Nikki," Jack said patiently. "About how to help her."

"Uh . . ."

"Go on," Nikki urged. "Tell them you used the time to find out what a great kisser I am."

"It's a long and complicated process," Tom said.

"How can you *lie* like that?" she almost shrieked.

"I'll have to spirit walk a few more times to get to the bottom of this."

"Yeah? Well, you can make out with a hermit crab for your pains, chum."

"So," Tom finished cheerfully, "no need to wake up your wife."

"Oh." Jack bent over and picked up his book. "As you wish. She'll be relieved you're back. Is Nikki okay?"

"She's fine," Tom said.

"I'm *fine*? Buster, the next time I can touch you, I'm giving you *such* a kick in the balls. . . ."

"You missed supper—and lunch—but I can go get you something from the lodge."

"Not hungry," Tom replied. "That's fine, take off."

"Are you sure?" Jack was lingering by the doorway. "I don't think I've seen you eat since you've gotten here."

"Oh, I had some crackers on the plane. Now shoo."

"Good advice," Nikki snapped, and marched through the wall.

"I didn't mean *you*!" she heard him yell after her. Too bad.

CHAPTER ◆ TWELVE

She had avoided the lot of them by lurking—haunting—the other side of the island. And she'd learned a crucial thing: no matter how powerful the psychic was, a ghost could hide from him if she really wanted to. And she really wanted to.

But, after sulking for a couple of days she decided to go back to the lodge side, just to check on Cathy if nothing else. And there was nothing else. Certainly she'd never care if she ever saw Mr. Makeout again.

There were a number of coast guard boats tied off and quite a few people milling about the lodge. Another unmarked van was idling in the driveway, and something in a big bag was being loaded into it. Nikki had a sickening feeling she knew what it was. And why Cathy and Jack weren't there.

She carefully walked into their cabin only to find the

three of them sitting in odd postures. It took her a minute to put her finger on what they were doing, and then it hit her: they were waiting.

"It's about damn time!" Tom snapped by way of greeting. He had, more's the pity, put on a shirt today to go with his cutoffs. Then, to her friends: "She's here."

Cathy's eyes were rimmed in red; she looked like she'd been playing with the wrong color eyeliner. "Nikki, they found—they found you today."

"Yeah, I gathered from all the ruckus."

Silence. A dead silence, one might say. Then Cathy added timidly, "So I guess she can go on, now?"

"Go on *what*?" Nikki asked.

"Cathy and Jack think that now that your body's been found, there's no reason for you to keep haunting them."

"I'm not haunting them!" she yelled. "How many times do I have to say it? I'm stuck, but I'm not haunting. I *want* them to get on with their lives, crissake, what's it been, three months?"

"Four and a half," Tom corrected her.

"Right! My point! Tell 'em I said to get lost! Go back to their lives! Bye-bye, Charlie!"

Tom blinked, then turned to Cathy. "She says finding her body made no difference. She wants you to get back to your own lives. She wants you to leave."

"But—but she's still here."

"Yup," he agreed.

"Look, if I could poof on to heaven or the next plane or the next life or whatever, don't you think I would have by now? I think—don't tell them this—I think I'm stuck here because *they're stuck here. I'm not haunting this place,* they are."

"She thinks your refusal to move on is why she's trapped here."

"I told you not to tell them!" she howled.

"My God, that's awful," Cathy gasped. "But—but tell her we can't just leave her here in limbo like this."

"Then she's doomed," Tom said. "Sorry to sound dramatic, but there it is. She can't move on if you can't move on."

Cathy bit her lip and looked down at her lap. Jack patted her arm with one hand, and tapped the nightstand with the fingers of his other hand, an obnoxious habit he had when he was thinking about something difficult.

"Besides, she won't be alone," Tom added. "I'll stay here. You know, help her onto the next plane, all that stuff."

"What?" Nikki was appalled, intrigued, and appalled all over again. "You don't know what you're talking about."

"Oh—you will?" Cathy brightened. "You'll stay with her? That's different. I mean—now that they've found the body—there isn't anything else for us to do. At least she can see you, talk to you."

"Right! Well, half right. Good-bye! And take *him* with you."

"Shall we discuss your fee? Because—"

"No, no." Tom waved that away. "The fee you already paid is more than I make in six months. That's fine."

"Well." Cathy bit her lip again and looked at her husband. "I guess we'd better pack."

Nikki walked back outside before Tom could hear

149

something she might regret. They were doing what she wanted, right? They were

(abandoning)

leaving her, right? It's what she wanted all along, to have a chance to

(be alone)

pick up the pieces, to let them

(live)

get back to their lives.

So how come she felt so shitty?

CHAPTER ◆ THIRTEEN

They packed. Took the van. Flew away. The other van (she assumed it was the coroner's van, if such a tiny island had such a thing) left. The coast guard left. Everybody left.

And now, finally, new guests were coming. She supposed that was a good thing, for the lodge at least. But she sure didn't like seeing strangers in what she thought of as Cathy and Jack's place. Guests who never knew she had existed, and certainly didn't care either way.

And she got what she wanted, right? Cathy and Jack had moved on. Her body had been found, identified, claimed, and, by now, buried next to her parents in the Hastings Cemetery. Everything was as fine as could be, under the circumstances. Right? She'd missed her own funeral, but who'd want to go to that anyway? Right?

Tom stayed. And because he was the only one she could

talk to, she swallowed her anger and started speaking to him again.

"So, did they get back okay?" she asked.

"It speaks!" he cried. He had sat down in one of the chairs and was pulling off his sandals; now he threw them in the corner and leaped to his feet. "Is it Halloween already?"

"Har-de-har-har. I was just wondering if my friends made it back okay."

"They're fine. Do you know how long I've been waiting for you to get over your mad-on? A damned month!"

"Oh, it hasn't been that long."

He muttered something. It sounded like "fucking dead people."

"What?"

"Spirits have no sense of time. At all."

"Oh. Well, this spirit doesn't, anyway."

"And why were you mad, anyway? Was it so awful that I liked spending time with you and wanted to do more of it?"

"I just think you should have told Jack the truth, that's all."

"That I spent half a day making out with you instead of doing my job?"

She giggled; she couldn't help it. He looked so aggrieved. "Maybe that *is* your job, American Gigolo."

"Sure. Right." He went to the bed, sat on it, became Lotus-Tom, and then Ghost-Tom stood up out of him. "So!" he said cheerfully, carefully climbing down (she could relate—if you moved too fast, you went *under* the cabin) and approaching her. "How about another kiss for your favorite psychic medium?"

"Did you say psychic or psychotic? And how about not?" She fended him off with a hand under his chin, trying not to giggle. "Is that all you've been thinking about? Being a ghost and making out?"

"Well, yeah," he admitted, knocking her hand away and grabbing for her, causing them to fall through the chair, the wall, and into the bathroom. "Pretty much."

"Have I mentioned I really like you shirtless? In fact, you should go shirtless all the time. Pantsless, too."

"Ditto." Their clothes (were the clothes incorporeal, too? must be) went flying (through the bathroom wall!), and she was kissing him with wild kisses, kissing him the way a desert survivor drank water, kissing him and loving being touched, being caressed, being groped. He wanted her at least as badly as she wanted him, so there weren't any flowers or candles or tenderness, just two bodies urgently trying to get into the same place.

She groaned as he entered her, but when he gritted "sorry," she responded by wrapping her legs around his waist and pushing back.

"Sorry, save your sorry and fuck me," she muttered, and his hand slapped the tile beside her head and curled into a white-knuckled fist, and he shivered over her.

"Better not say that again," he groaned, "or we'll be done right now."

"So one of your powers isn't stamina?"

He groaned again and laughed at the same time, and their stomachs slapped against each other as they quickened to some internal beat, a song only they could hear. She wouldn't come, of course, she was the kind of woman who needed at least ten minutes of foreplay, but that was all right, because just being touched, being with him, was enough for—

She came. She came so hard she thought the top of her head would come off. And he was right there with her the whole time, and he never stopped touching her, and she never wanted it to stop, not any of it, not ever.

CHAPTER ◆ FOURTEEN

"Look at this," she said, picking her shirt up and putting it back on. "Is it a real shirt? Why do I have to put it back on?"

"You don't."

"Funny. But why do we even have clothes? Are they ghost clothes? Why am I always in this shirt and these shorts?"

"Because that's how you saw yourself—casually dressed, comfortable, attractive."

She touched her hair and tried to look modest. "And you said the dead have no sense of time—how come?"

"You're not ruled by clocks like the living. How long have we been stuck in that shitty bathroom, making love?"

"Half an hour?" she guessed, stepping into her shorts.

He looked wounded. "All day. We missed the lunch bell and the supper bell."

"Oh. Well, it was a great day," she assured him. "Don't you want to go eat?"

"I'll stay here with you."

"Both of you?" she asked, a little creeped out. Here was Ghost-Tom, strolling around naked, and here was Lotus-Tom, sitting like someone frozen to the bed.

"I can only touch you in this form," he said quietly.

"Yeah, but Tom, you've got to take care of your—your living body."

He shrugged, indifferent. "Want to go for a walk?"

Yep. Definitely broken. "Uh, sure. But it's no problem to wait until you've eaten. Hell, I probably won't even notice if you leave for half an hour; it'll seem like thirty seconds to—"

There was a rap on the hut door, which Tom ignored. Nikki, being the kind of person who always had to answer the phone or the door, stuck her head through the wall and said, "It's the manager. Don't you want to answer it?"

"No."

"But it might be important."

"Is he holding phone slips?"

She peeked again. "Yes."

"It's just job offers."

"Job offers?"

"Jobbbb offffers, arrrre youuuuuu haaaaaving trrrrouble hearrrring meeee?"

"Very funny. You're turning down work to hang out with the dead girl?"

He shrugged; a maddening habit, but eloquent. "Your friends paid me plenty."

"But still. Don't you want to get back to work?"

He looked at her. "No."

She was surprised to discover that a ghost could blush. "Oh."

"So how about that walk?"

She smiled. "Sure. I'd love a walk. I can show you all the places I've been haunting."

He laughed. "Two ghosts, no waiting. Wouldn't the tourists just shit?"

"What if one of them is special, like you?"

"Nobody's like me," he said simply. Not bragging; stating fact.

"Well, that's the truth."

"Say it twice," he said smugly, and held out an arm, and escorted her through the wall.

CHAPTER ◆ FIFTEEN

"Tom . . ."

"Mmmm?"

They were in the pool, walking around in the deep end holding hands. It was a riot! They both ran and jumped to get momentum, and here they were. Nikki kept holding her breath from force of habit, then remembering and letting it out with a whoosh, which Tom found endlessly amusing.

"This has been a great couple of days—"

"Three weeks," he corrected.

"Right. And it's been awesome. Don't get me wrong. But . . . when are you going to go?"

He frowned at her. "Go?"

"Yeah, you know. Hop a plane, get back to you life. You must have one."

"A plane?"

"A life."

"I like it here," he said, sounding wounded.

"Well, yeah, but Tom—you can't just stay here indefinitely with me."

"Why not?"

"Why *not*? What do you mean, why not? You just can't! It's not like we're a normal couple. I'm dead, for crying out loud."

"So?"

She stopped walking and pulled her hand out of his. A pair of legs appeared in the shallow end and she had a *Jaws*-eye view of the swimmer.

She ignored it and addressed the (rather large) problem at hand. "Let me get this straight. My problem was Jack and Cathy couldn't move on, and now it's that you can't move on? You're not eating, you're not taking work, you're in limbo just like me."

"Just like you."

"No, Tom, that's a *bad* thing. That's why you're so goddamned skinny: You escape your life by hanging out with ghosts. And you lose track of time, just like I do. Have you considered the fact that one of these days you might just starve to death?"

"That would be awful," he said without a shred of conviction.

"Oh, come on! That's not a plan, is it? A seriously fucked-up plan?"

"Would it be so bad if it was?"

"Tom, you have a life! You can't just—just throw it away so we can hold hands and watch the sunset. Come on!"

"Can't we?" he asked quietly.

"You. Have. A. Life. This." She gestured to the legs flailing above them. "Is not. A life. You're alive! You'll be dead soon enough, even if you live to be eighty."

"It's different for everyone," he said, still so quietly she had to strain to hear him.

"What?"

"It's—I think it's whatever you can imagine. If you see harps and angels, that's where you go. If you see hell, that's where you go. If you think you have unfinished business, you stay here. The afterlife—it can be anything. Anything at all. And I don't know if—what if I live to the end of my life and go somewhere else? What if I can't find you again?"

"Are you saying—are you saying that you love me and want to be with me?" Because he hadn't said it. She hadn't, either.

They'd had sex all over the island—once on top of the bar in front of six patrons who couldn't see them.

They'd talked about things, private things, they had never told anyone.

The only thing they hadn't talked about was the future. Because, of course, there wasn't one. Not for them, anyway.

"Because I—" Love you, she started to say, then stopped. Wasn't that making things worse? How could he move on if she told him? And that was the worst of it: four months ago (or six, or eight, or whatever) there had been one ghost trapped on the island.

Now there were two.

"Of course I don't love you, how could I love you?" he cried, and his voice was bitter, so bitter. "You're the same as all the others, why can't I think of you like all the others? You're just one of *them*."

"Them?" But she knew. Sure she knew. Here was Tom, spirit walking with a dead woman because that was better than anything else he had planned for that day, that month, that year. And here was why.

"Just a—just another ghost who distracted my dad. I couldn't get any fucking attention from that guy unless I was working. Do you know what it's like to be eight years old and totally jaded on the human condition, but still want your dad's approval more than anything?"

"No," she said quietly. "I don't."

"Well, it fucking sucks. And you—you! You're just the same, just another dead person who only cares about what she can get so she can move on, just me-me-me, and never mind that maybe my dad and I should have had a life, never mind that there was never enough money in the bank account to satisfy him, there was always one more job, one more person to help, never mind Christmas, never mind my birthday, we gotta drop everything because some idiot didn't look both ways and got creamed crossing the street, and now she's freaking out about not telling her husband about the new checking account."

He paused and gulped in a new breath (not that he needed to in this form, but old habits died hard and if she didn't believe that, just look around her), and she waited for more tirade, but he deflated like a stuck tire. "I guess that's all I have. Your turn."

"Uh, I've got nothing like that."

"Nobody has."

"Now who's being self-involved?" she teased.

"I'm sorry for what I said," he said dully.

"It's all right. I know a lie when I hear one."

He met her gaze with difficulty. "I love you. I'd die for you."

"I love you, too, and I absolutely forbid it. No dying allowed."

They linked hands and walked through the pool wall, through the earth, and up into the sunlight. "You had to work on Christmas?" she finally asked.

"Yes."

"Where was your mom?"

"Dead. She died having me. She was the first ghost I ever saw. She—" He swallowed and she heard the dry click in his throat. "She tried to get me away from my dad, tried to talk me into running away to my aunt's. She wasn't afraid he'd hurt me, just that he'd . . . use me up, you know?"

"Yeah."

"But he was my dad."

She knew. You could never walk away from your parents; they trapped you with sticky webs made of love. You were the fly to their spider. But they only ate you because they loved you.

"Nikki, where's your family? You seemed so concerned about Cathy and Jack—"

"They're my family. I was an only child, and my parents died when I was a freshman in college. Cathy sort of adopted me, you know? We've been friends for a long time."

"What happened to your folks?"

They were walking through the sand now, headed for his cabin. "Well . . ."

"Is it horrible? It's horrible, isn't it?" His fingers tightened over hers. "You can tell me. There isn't a thing I haven't heard, honey, you can trust me on that one."

"No, it's not that horrible, but you'll make a big thing out of it."

"Because it's horrible!"

"It's *not*. Okay, calm down, I'll tell you. Just—don't read into it. It's not a big thing. Okay?"

"*Mmm*. Tell me."

"Well, I was the first person in my family to go to college, right? In fact, I thought that was my name for a while; my mom never introduced me as Nikki or Nicole, it was always 'This is The First Person In Our Family To Go To College.' You could actually *hear* the capital letters.

"So, anyway, we didn't have a pot to piss in, so I got a scholarship and a part-time job, started at the U of M that fall, blah-blah. My parents were so proud; I'd finally made my other name a reality. Then I get a call from Mom's neighbor: big car accident, they're both in the hospital, some dipwad drunk driver ran a red.

"So, I call the hospital—Abbott—and my mom's conscious, but my dad's in surgery and can't talk to me. And my mom's all, 'Don't come, don't come, we're fine, it's finals week there, right?' I mean, she knew my schedule better than I did.

"But I was all, 'Come on, Mom, you guys are hurt, I'll come see you.' And then Mom tells the biggest lie of all: It's nothing, we're fine. We'll call you when we get discharged, come see us after you take your tests.

"And, of course, they died. Dad wasn't in surgery; he was in a coma. Mom died on the operating table. She cheated me out of saying good-bye because she didn't want me to miss my exams. Stupid! Like the school wouldn't have let me take them after the funerals. But Mom didn't know anything about college. Because I was—"

"The First Person In Your Family To Go To College."

"Yeah."

"So. You weren't there for them when they needed you."

"Yes, and I felt tricked and betrayed, and do not be going and making something out of this. It's got nothing to do with what's happening now."

"No, of course not. I'm sure that's not significant in any way."

They were cuddling on the bed now, looking up at the ceiling. Nikki wondered why they bothered—they were incorporeal, they could sleep outside. Heck, they could sleep in a grove of trees and never get bitten by a bug. But old habits.

Lotus-Tom was sitting in a chair across the room. She was used to having two Toms around by now, and scarcely noticed him. "So, back to the business at hand. I love you. And you love me."

"Yes," he said, sounding—could it be? Happy? Well, she'd fix that in a hurry. "I love you and you love me."

"So. You have to go."

"No."

"Yes. Tom, you have to. There's—there's no hope for us. I'm stuck here and you have a life, and if you stay, I'll walk into the ocean and never come back."

"I can't leave you."

"You better. Because I'm not going to have your death on my conscience, Skinny."

"And what kind of a life am I going back to? Being at the beck and call of crackpots?"

"They're not all crackpots," she said quietly. "Some of them need your help. For some of them, you're the *only* one who can help them. You can't turn your back on your life's work for me."

"It's my father's life's work," he said bitterly, "and just watch me."

"Tom. Isn't it bad enough that I'm in limbo? You have to be, too?"

"I won't let you send me away."

"Yes, you will. You know why. I didn't get a chance to say good-bye once, and it's cast a shadow over my life—and death. You have to let me go, just like I have to let you go. That's what all this *is*. There's a lesson to be learned, and I'm by God going to *learn* it this time, you know?"

"No," he said again. He sounded fine, but she could see tears trickling down his cheeks; how they shone in the moonlight! He squeezed her, held her, hugged her hard. "No, no, no."

"Yes."

"Yes."

"Tomorrow."

"No. A week," he begged. "Another month."

"You think this will be easier in a month?" To keep him company, she was crying, too. "It'll never be easier than it is tomorrow—only harder. You have to go. You have to let me go. And I have to let you go. It's the only way we'll be free."

"Freedom is fucking overrated," he said, almost shouted.

"Don't lie to me, Tom. I can spot one a mile away. Now ask me why."

He groaned. "I know why."

"Now ask me how I can let you go."

He picked up her hand, kissed the knuckles. "I know that, too."

They held each other all night and Nikki thought she had never cried so long or so hard, or seen a man cry at all.

And she thought: *your heart can still break when you're dead, oh yes.*

CHAPTER ◆ SIXTEEN

She waited until he fell asleep, and left. She couldn't watch him leave. If she did, she would weaken, beg him to stay, happily watch as he indifferently starved himself to death, had a heart attack from potassium deficiency, toppled over in bed, and suffocated because he had no one to watch his body. *Whatever, just die and be with me.* Except there were no guarantees that he *would* be with her. And just because her life had been cut short, why should his?

No, she wanted him to live for a hundred years, five hundred, just like she wanted Cathy and Jack and their baby to live for a hundred years. A hundred years at least.

She was going over the same ground again and again (literally; she was on the south side of the island again) and tried to think of something else. Anything else.

She closed her eyes and thought of Tom. His smile, his rare beautiful smile. His long fingers. His eyes, so wounded and so bright. His skinny legs and bony arms; God, he was scrawny. In her heart's eye, she loved it all, even the way he nibbled on his hangnails when he was distracted.

Tom. You'd better be drinking a milkshake right now. You'd better be—well, if not happy, at least resigned. Happiness will come. It's got to. It—

She opened her eyes.

And managed to just stop herself from screaming in surprise.

The beach was gone. The ocean was gone. She was in someone's living room.

She looked around wildly. Yes, the beach was gone. Yes: couch, coffee table, end tables, chairs . . . this was a living room. She walked over to the window and looked out: traffic streamed by below. And—she *knew* this place. This was Commonwealth Avenue. Boston, Massachusetts.

Boston? But that was where—

She heard keys jingling, locks clacking, and turned around in time to see the door swing open and Tom walk inside, white-faced with fatigue.

Their eyes locked. They spoke in less than romantic unison: "What the hell are *you* doing here?"

"This is my apartment," he said, dropping his bag. On his foot, she noticed, but he didn't notice. "This is where you told me to go."

"But—but—but—but—" She had made him go. She had insisted he set them free. And now she was free. Free to go where she wanted.

What had he said, what had his unique vision of the afterlife been?

He slammed the door, curled into Lotus-Tom right there in the living room.

(It's whatever you can imagine.)

Jumped out of Lotus-Tom, raced to her. Kissed her until she thought they'd both topple through the window.

(If you see harps and angels, that's where you go. If you see hell, that's where you go. If you think you have unfinished business, you stay here.)

"I love you, I love you," he was saying, raining kisses on her face, "I love you, but I'm going to choke you for sending me away, I love you."

(The afterlife—it can be anything. Anything at all.)

"I've got some bad news for you," she said, kissing him back.

He held her at arm's length. "What?"

"Well, you have to eat more."

"Done. What's the bad news?"

"Your apartment's haunted. You're my afterlife."

"Oh, that," he said. "Luckily, I happen to be a psychic." And kissed her some more.

HOT SUMMER BITES

Nina Bangs

◆ PROLOGUE

"Cosmic troublemaker test-time." Sparkle Stardust let the words resonate in her soul. Fine, so she didn't have a soul, but they still resonated. She loved it when a young troublemaker she'd mentored got a chance to show his stuff.

Deimos looked suspicious. He'd propped his massive six-feet-plus of solid muscle against the candy store's closed door and crossed his arms over his broad chest.

"First, a progress report." She popped a black jellybean into her mouth. Chocolate was a more sensual treat, but jellybeans helped her think. "I agreed to mentor you because I saw the promise of a troublemaker who could develop into a sexual manipulator almost as powerful as me." She thought about that. "Of course, even *I* sometimes make a mistake."

Deimos's gaze skittered away from Sparkle as he fumbled with the doorknob behind him.

"Forget it. You're not leaving until I'm ready for you to leave." Sparkle hopped off the stool she kept behind the counter and strolled to the door. "I've given you all my knowledge, and now it's time for you to produce." She held up her hand before he could lay a lame excuse on her.

"You're not a virgin anymore, so don't try to use that to wiggle out of your duty. As far as I can see, you haven't made even one attempt to mess with anyone's sex life. If you fail, then I fail in the eyes of the troublemaker world." She stood on tiptoe in her Manolo Blahnik stilettos and glared at him eyeball to chin. "I will *not* be humiliated. Ergo, you will *not* fail me. Got it?"

Deimos ran his hand nervously over his shaved head. "Yes, ma'am."

Sparkle frowned as she stared past him out the store's window. "Jeez, you just scared a little kid away who wanted to spend his candy money. Go stand somewhere else and try not to loom. You know, the bald head, the tattoos, the biker-dude look, it's not helping me sell candy."

Deimos shrugged. "Action heroes need to be scary-looking so the bad guys will respect them."

Okay, Sparkle was officially pissed. "Yeah, well, there're a bunch of preschoolers outside who respect you to death."

Sparkle sighed. It was a good thing she really didn't need the money from the store. Sweet Indulgence was just a front for her real purpose—to foment sexual chaos by matching up people who were totally wrong for each other in every way except between the sheets.

Her setup was brilliant. The candy store was right outside Live the Fantasy, an adult theme park where people could act out their fantasies, childhood or otherwise. It was the possibility for "otherwise" that interested her.

"Here's the deal. In exactly ten minutes Kristin Hughes will check into the Castle of Dark Dreams. She's an investigative reporter who's gotten wind that some of the fantasies offered in the park are sexual in nature—don't I wish. Anyway, she'll be poking around looking for the sex." Sparkle's smile was a slow slide of wicked anticipation. "You, Deimos, will see that she finds it."

His amber eyes rounded in panic. "How?"

"That's part of the test, silly." She contemplated the perfection of her nails—Luscious Lust nail color, no chips, no broken edges. It didn't get much better than that. "Taurin just got back from a fruitless search for his long-lost brother. He's feeling pretty down."

Deimos's horrified expression said he knew what was coming.

"To pass the test and graduate, you have to hook those two up." Sparkle knew her eyes gleamed with the intensity of the true zealot.

"But he's a vampire."

Sparkle clapped her hands. "Exactly. It'll be a deliciously evil and incredibly difficult test. If you pass it, you'll be ready to fly." She paused to study his petulant expression. "Well, maybe not fly. But at least you'll be up to a fast walk."

"I don't want to do it." From his narrowed amber eyes to his pouty lower lip, Deimos was Mr. Sulky. "I'm a supernatural being with lots of power. I should be doing what other cosmic troublemakers do, wreaking havoc throughout the universe, stuff like that."

Sparkle tried to look sympathetic, but she oozed sarcasm. She couldn't help it; he made her crazy. "I feel your pain, Deimos. It's tough being conflicted."

"Huh?"

"I mean, do you choose good or evil? Should you be an action hero who does boring good stuff or a cosmic trouble-maker who enjoys the rush of creating spectacularly evil events?" Sparkle didn't leave any doubt on which side of the good-or-evil fence she perched.

Deimos furrowed his brow.

Amazing. Sparkle had never seen anyone actually do that. "So what's your choice?" She wasn't worried. Anyone with a brain in his head would choose to be a troublemaker. Okay, so maybe she *should* worry. She'd forgotten about the pre-requisite brain.

Deimos's expression cleared. He grinned. "I'll be both."

She dropped the sympathetic look. "Not possible."

"Sure it is." He punched the air to emphasize his convic-tion, and a little old lady peering at the chocolate display in the window ran away screaming. "First I'll make bad stuff happen, then I'll become an action hero and rush in to save everybody."

"That is so . . ." Words couldn't describe how pissed-off she was. "Forget the action-hero crap. It's time to prove you can be a cosmic troublemaker."

Mr. Sulky was back. "I'm not going to hook up Taurin and this Kristin Hughes. I want to do really cool stuff, like Ganymede does."

Time to take off the gloves. "You have no idea how lucky you are that I plucked you out of the newbie pile. You want to be like Ganymede and run around laying waste to the universe? Fine, in ten thousand years come back and we'll talk about it. But right now? You make your choice. You don't want to do things my way, then get your butt back to Beginners' Central. I hear they're looking for a troublemaker to take over Septicanus's job. He was in charge of constipation and other related miseries of the world. Interested?"

Deimos's expression was so horrified that Sparkle would've laughed if she weren't so mad.

"Okay, I'll take the test." He looked miserable and a little lost. "Uh, any ideas to get me started?"

She sighed. You had to have so much patience with the young ones. "First, let Taurin know what Kristin's up to. Then get them together. Make sure he understands that if she discovers nonhuman entities have found a haven in the park, she'll write about it, and his cozy home will be only a distant memory. If I know our boy, he'll take it from there. Vampires hate publicity."

What else would further the cause? "Oh, and you might want to plan a beach party. A midnight beach party. Next Monday would be good. Taurin's off on Mondays, and it's a full moon. Think of the sensual possibilities—moonlight shining on the water, the sound of the waves, and the breeze drifting over heated bodies. The whole setup screams sex."

"Uh-huh." Deimos looked doubtful.

"Do it." She'd finish off by throwing him a little incentive. "Who knows, you might even get a chance to use your action-hero skills before the week is done."

His eyes lit up. "Oh, wow. You think so? Guess I'd better get started." He yanked the door open and was gone.

Sparkle smiled. Men were so easily manipulated. If nothing else, the week should be good for lots of laughs. And if Deimos screwed things up too badly, she'd step in to help Kristin and Taurin see they were fated for each other.

Her smile turned wicked. Of course, she'd forgotten to tell Deimos one little thing: Kristin and Taurin already knew each other, and their hate was mutual. God, she loved her work.

CHAPTER ◆ ONE

Taurin Veris thought about ripping out Deimos's throat. How long had it been since he'd done something just for the hell of it? Too long.

Yeah, but then he'd have to listen to everyone bitching at him. So he controlled the urge. Deimos trailed him out of the Castle of Dark Dreams and into the Texas night.

Taurin gave the "No, uh-uh, won't do it, definitely not" routine another shot. "Look, I need downtime. I just got back from searching for Dacian in some of the crappiest places on earth and came up empty. So I don't want to hear about any damn reporter. Get someone else to deal with her."

"Everyone else is busy." Deimos caught up with him. "Sparkle thinks she could be trouble."

"Then it's true, because Sparkle wrote the book on trouble." If he walked faster, would Deimos give up?

"No, you don't get it. She's an investigative reporter, and she's here rooting around for a sensational story. She got a tip that Live the Fantasy does all kinds of weird sexual fantasies."

"And I'm supposed to care why?" This was an *adult* theme park. Rumors of sex would sell more tickets. It was all good. Why was Deimos bent out of shape?

The whites of Deimos's eyes showed. All the way around. "But what happens if she accidentally finds out there're a bunch of nonhuman entities living here? You'll all have to move."

That got his attention. He was happy here, and he'd be damned if he'd let another nosy snoop ruin that. It had happened once, but it wouldn't happen again. "So what's Sparkle suggest?"

Taurin usually enjoyed his nightly walk. He could take a look at what was going on in the park, or if he wanted something different, he could cross Seawall Boulevard and walk along the beach. He never tired of the Gulf. Galveston was more home to him than any other place had been in six hundred years. And he intended it to stay that way.

"Keep her busy. Show her around the park. Don't give her time to do much poking." Deimos got more enthusiastic with each word. "I'm planning a midnight beach party for next Monday. Eric, Brynn, and Conall will all be off." He grinned. "You can bring the reporter with you. Let her see everything's cool."

"*You're* planning a beach party?" The only thing Deimos ever planned was his next action-hero move. "Never mind. About this showing-her-around thing, I have a job. I can't spend all week keeping her nose pointed in the right direction. And what about during the day? Who's going to keep her out of trouble then?"

Deimos looked triumphant. "Sparkle took care of that. She told Holgarth about the problem, and he cleared your slate for the week. Now you can spend all the time you want with her. And they just hired a new guy to help with the tours and stuff during the day. A wereshark. Needs to be near the water. He'll keep her busy while you're down. I have her name and room number here somewhere." He rooted around in his pocket until he found a piece of paper. "She's in room 218, and her name's Kristin Hughes."

"Where the hell does Sparkle get off going to Holgarth about . . ." Taurin rounded on Deimos, every sense alert. "Did you say Kristin Hughes?"

Deimos nodded, a little uncertain now. "Yeah. You know her?"

Taurin grew still, that completely motionless state that allowed him to hear even the flow of his victim's blood. It was the silence of a hunting predator. "Oh, I know her all right. Tell Sparkle I'll keep the lady so distracted she won't know which way is up." Who would've thought he'd cross paths with her again? But it looked like the bitch was back.

Deimos nodded happily and hurried away. Probably afraid Taurin would change his mind if he hung around. No chance of that. He turned back toward the castle, his walk forgotten.

First he'd tell Holgarth his plans, and the wizard could pass it on to the others. Taurin would have to meet this wereshark. Make sure they were on the same page. Kristin and the shark would be perfect together. They had lots in common—a killer instinct and a taste for blood. Okay, so he had a taste for blood, too. But he liked to think that he retained some semblance of humanity.

Then he'd pay a visit to Ms. Hughes and welcome her to the Castle of Dark Dreams. So she thought Live the Fantasy was all about sex? He'd give her so much sex to write about that she wouldn't even notice if Holgarth whacked her over the head with his wand and turned her into a leech. Oh, wait, she already was one. Taurin knew his smile showed lots of fang.

Kristin Hughes wrote two kinds of stories—the impact of global warming on the United States' economy kind, and werewolves roaming the Minnesota forests kind. Serious and fluff. The fluff paid better. She was in the Castle of Dark Dreams looking for some heavy-duty fluff.

She lay sprawled across the crimson bedspread of her decadent four-poster bed, which fit right in with the rest of her authentic-looking castle chamber. The room was all massive dark wood, rich fabrics, and jewel-tone colors. It screamed erotic. A far cry from stumbling through the Minnesota underbrush looking for werewolves.

But she was after something much different here. A few days ago she'd gotten an anonymous e-mail claiming that the whole park was a sexual playground, not the G-rated, role-playing, fun-for-all place it advertised. She was here to dig up the truth, and if she was really lucky, she'd find kinky sex around every corner. Kinky sex in unexpected places sold like crazy.

Only one possible dark cloud lurked on her horizon. The last time she'd done a story in Texas, she'd stirred up real trouble for herself. She'd written an article on a group of vampire wannabes in San Antonio. Vampires? How twisted was that?

She'd paid a mole to infiltrate the group and feed her info. He'd made her think they'd welcome the publicity. Most gatherings of the strange-and-unusual were all about getting attention. Uh, why else would anyone claim he was a vampire?

Anyway, once the public read her stuff, the curious descended on the weird group. All the publicity scared the vamps off, and they left town toting their coffins behind them. How was she to know they wanted to keep everything hush-hush?

Kristin frowned. Now came the bad part. For months afterward, this crazy guy named Veris—maybe that wasn't even his real name—had made her life hell. He'd found all kinds of creative ways to put a hurting on her career, and he'd made sure she knew it was payback for the San Antonio thing. None of her investigative skills helped her ID him. Once he stopped, she swore she'd never do another Texas story. But here she was. This was too good to pass up.

Kristin opened her Live the Fantasy brochure and tried to decide where she'd start. They had fantasies going on in the castle right now. It would make sense to take in one of those first. Pretty convenient to have a theme park attraction and hotel all rolled into one. Now or tomorrow night? She was pretty tired after her flight. Maybe she'd wait until—

A knock interrupted her train of thought. Kristin frowned. She wasn't expecting anyone. Climbing from the comfort of her bed, she went to the door and opened it.

Oh. My. God. The man leaning against the doorjamb with arms crossed over his chest was . . . was . . . *Okay, need oxygen to keep brain working. Breathe in, breathe out, breathe in, breathe out.* Basic description—a little over six feet tall, dark shaggy hair, dark do-me eyes, shirtless, worn jeans riding low on hips, shirtless, scuffed biker boots, and shirtless.

"Hey, sweetcheeks. I'm Taurin, the castle handyman. Right now I'm Air-conditioning Man, here to save you from a hot night." Pregnant pause. "Unless a hot night excites you."

"Air-conditioning? It's fine." Now for the not-so-basic description: broad, bare chest, powerful pecs, impressive abs, and would he notice if she pulled off her top? Yeah, he would. But the sweat wending a meandering path between her breasts was getting on her nerves. Maybe her air-conditioning wasn't so fine.

"Oh, I don't know about that." He strode past her to the thermostat and stood staring at it. A loud clanking noise came from the air vents and the air shut down. "See. I got here just in time."

"You betcha." Woo-hoo, would you look at that butt—

round, tight, and totally drool-worthy. She'd need a bib by the time he fixed the air-conditioning.

"Lucky for you I have my tool belt loaded." His voice lowered to a husky murmur. "I have a tool for every need. Long, strong, and able to get into tight places."

"Uh-huh." Was it physically possible for her tongue to get tangled in her vocal cords? Must be, because she sure was having trouble talking. She dropped her gaze. Yep, there was his tool belt. And his screwdriver had this big, firm, strong-looking handle that was so . . . so . . . symbolic.

He pulled the cover off the thermostat and did some fiddling with the innards. "Here for a vacation?"

"Sort of." Now that she'd gotten over her initial shock, she started to wonder about a hotel employee showing up shirtless. Unless . . . unless the castle was totally into sexual excess. Then a hot handyman would make lots of sense. The thought, admittedly out there, cheered her. "I'm a freelance writer, and I thought I'd do a story"—read exposé—"about the park."

He continued tinkering with the thermostat. Hmm, the noise had been in the vents, so she didn't see why he was fooling with the thermostat. But what did she know about air conditioners?

"You should start with a Castle of Dark Dreams fantasy." He glanced at his watch while she glanced at the play of smooth muscle across his back. "I'm almost done here, and then I can quit for the night. How about we go down to the great hall together, and I'll introduce you to the park's fantasy world? Call it a welcome gift."

Kristin considered his "gift." Why not experience her first fantasy with him? If she was looking for the sexual underbelly of this park, he was as good a place to start as any. Darkly sensual and wickedly tempting, he would make a perfect guide to all the sinfully delicious secrets of Live the Fantasy.

In fact, if she worked things right, she might be able to keep him for the whole week. *Whoa, rein in stampeding lust.* She'd have lots of fun researching this article, but it was still all about the job. Besides, he'd only offered to guide her through one fantasy, not strip off her clothes and then make wild, planet-exploding love with her.

She sighed. Okay, so that was *her* fantasy. She'd lived most of her life in small-town North Dakota where absolutely nothing unusual ever happened. Can we say boring with a big, bold capital *B*?

Mom and Dad were great people, but they were convinced that once she reached the age when her hormonal tide was at flood stage, she'd slip from their grasp and be swept away by waves of sexual depravity. Her parents had kept her on such a tight leash she still had a collar mark around her neck, metaphorically speaking of course.

So when she finally escaped to college and afterward to the big, bad city, Kristin probably overcompensated a little by searching out stories that didn't reek of ordinary small-town America. And anything that promised kinky sex had her instant attention.

"Sounds like an offer I can't turn down." She slipped her sandals on. No matter what might happen during the fantasy, Kristin's cup of vicarious sensuality was full. "Let's go."

He guided her out the door and closed it behind him. "Why don't you go down to the great hall, and I'll meet you there. I have to drop my tool belt in my room and put on a shirt."

"Sure." She wanted to know about that shirt, but decided not to ask. He might actually have a good reason for not wearing one. Kristin liked her take on his shirtless state better—namely that the castle was dedicated to sex, so she'd be meeting shirtless, hot bods around every decadent corner. Ignoring the elevator, she headed for the winding stone stairs.

Taurin watched from narrowed eyes as she disappeared down the stairs. She'd been a surprise. He'd never seen Kristin Hughes. In San Antonio, she'd sent someone else in to do her dirty work, and he'd pictured a dried-up, vicious hag, because . . . Fine, so a dried-up, vicious hag would be easier to hate.

Not that he hated her less just because she had long black hair, big blue eyes, and pouty lips that would drive a man crazy if she chose to put them on any part of his body. And just because she had great breasts, an excellent ass, and long, long legs didn't affect his feelings for her in the least. He'd bet she was dried up and vicious on the inside.

He took the elevator down to the floor below the great hall. The dungeon was there, along with all the vampires' rooms. No windows, so it was the only part of the castle that sunlight couldn't reach. Taurin slipped on a black

T-shirt and was on his way up to the great hall when he met Eric.

At one time he'd thought Eric was responsible for his brother's death, but then he'd found out that Dacian wasn't dead at all. Now he was glad to have Eric on his side. "She's upstairs waiting for me. I'm doing a fantasy with her. How about if I take your part this time?"

Eric raised one sardonic brow. "You want to be Eric the Evil?"

Taurin knew his smile didn't reach his eyes. "No, I want to be Taurin the Hot, able to fulfill a certain nosy freelance writer's sexual fantasies so she won't have time to notice that some of us have fangs or alternate forms."

"No problem. But don't use my plaid. I'm the only Highland vampire in the house."

"Your plaid's safe. I'm going traditional. Long black cape and . . . Well, guess that's it. A long black cape. Nothing else." Taurin tried to ratchet down his anticipatory rush. He shouldn't be looking forward to this so much, because that gave her an importance she didn't deserve.

"Taking it over the top, aren't you? Be careful." Eric looked a little uneasy. "Holgarth may be a lawyer as well as a wizard, but we don't need him wearing his attorney's hat to defend you on an indecent exposure charge."

"The woman wants a sensational story, so I'll give her what she wants." Taurin put on his mock-shock expression. "*Indecent* exposure? Hey, anything I expose isn't just decent, it's damn good."

Call him cynical, but down through the centuries he'd learned that most women were all about externals. Show a female a great body, and she was all over it. Emotions were just so much excess baggage. Granted, he'd pretty much stuck with female night feeders since he became vampire, but he'd bet human females had the same take on sex. "And if she comes unglued, we can make sure she doesn't remember a thing."

Eric still looked unconvinced. "So let's say you give her what she wants and then don't wipe her memory before she leaves the castle. What's going to happen when her story hits the street?"

Taurin shrugged. "I'm going to be her source for all things sexual, so if I say she made everything up, who's going to believe her? I'll make sure she doesn't leave with any proof, and I can point to the stories she's done on vampires and werewolves to show that she's into sensationalism." The payoff would be huge. "Holgarth might even be able to sue her ass." Uh-oh, shouldn't have mentioned any body parts, because no matter how much he hated Kristin Hughes, she had a behind that lent itself to vibrant visuals.

Eric laughed. "Go for it. I'll walk up with you and take a look at her."

Once in the great hall, Taurin spotted Kristin talking with Holgarth. Not unexpected. Holgarth took his duty of greeting and irritating new guests seriously. Taurin hurried to reach her before the wizard drove her from the castle. He didn't want that to happen.

Logically, that would be a *good* thing to happen. But logic had nothing to do with his feelings for Kristin. He wanted her to stay because . . . he wanted the personal joy of knowing he'd deprived her of the biggest story of her life. Namely, that the castle was run by a vampire, a former demon of sensual desire, and an immortal warrior.

And as a sidebar, he'd have the added pleasure of watching her rub shoulders with all kinds of nontraditional beings and not have a clue. The thought of how he intended to keep her distracted from the truth lurking right under her inquisitive nose triggered the slide of his fangs.

He frowned. At least he thought that's what triggered it. Sure, her green top dipped low enough to expose the smooth skin of her throat. But come on now, this was the throat of the hated Kristin Hughes, the woman who single-handedly chased him and eleven of his night-feeder friends out of San Antonio. No matter how bright and shiny her wrapping paper looked, inside the package beat a cold, cold heart.

"Nice," Eric murmured just before they joined Holgarth.

"Didn't notice." Taurin winced. Stupid lie. Not that he had anything against lying when the situation called for it, but denying the obvious would only make Eric suspicious. And the other vampire could make his life hell if he thought Taurin had any sexual interest in Kristin. Which he didn't. At all.

Eric cast him a considering look before turning his smile on Kristin. "Welcome to the Castle of Dark Dreams, Kristin. I'm Eric McNair. You'll meet my brothers, Brynn and Conall, during your fantasy. We all try to make sure everyone has a great experience while they're here. Taurin was just telling me about you. Has Holgarth filled you in on how the fantasies work?"

"Sort of." The crease between her spectacular blue eyes told Taurin that Holgarth had been busy spreading his own brand of goodness and light.

They needed a full-time damage-control team to follow the wizard around. As a meeter and greeter, Holgarth was really scary. Time to refocus her on who was important in this castle. *Him.* "I'll help you pick out your costume, and then I'll turn you over to someone else who'll get you ready for your personal fantasy."

She looked confused. "But I thought you'd stay with me."

Taurin hoped his smile wasn't as feral as it felt. "Start the fantasy without me. I'll catch up."

Holgarth harrumphed loudly to show his displeasure that someone had shifted attention away from his pompous self. He adjusted his tall conical hat, smoothed his fingers over his long pointed gray beard, and then dramatically swirled his gold-trimmed blue robe around himself. "I was telling Ms. Hughes that she's unlikely to find anything worth writing about here. We're all ordinary down-home folks trying to entertain the masses."

Eric turned away as he tried to stifle his bark of laughter.

Holgarth frowned at the strangled sounds Eric was making. "Of course, *I've* managed to rise above the ordinary. So if you ever feel the need for a truly Pulitzer-worthy story, I'll try to make time in my busy schedule to accommodate you."

"Uh, thanks. I guess." Kristin cast Taurin a frantic glance.

Before Holgarth could lay any lies on her, Taurin grabbed Kristin's hand and dragged her off to the costume room. "Tell me what you'd like to be. All our fantasies take place in a medieval setting. We have virgin bride costumes, slave girl costumes, queen's handmaiden costumes, sacrificial—"

"Vampire slayer costume."

"What?"

"I did research on the Castle of Dark Dreams, and I know that Eric the Evil takes the form of a vampire. So I want to be a slayer." She glanced around. "No offense, but all the women's costumes here whimper, 'I am doormat, see me grovel.'" She flipped through the costumes. "Sexist, sexist, sexist. The PC police need an anonymous call. Isn't there a queen's costume here somewhere?"

"We already have a queen." It was hard talking through gritted teeth. Crap and double crap. He'd been pulling for the slave girl costume. "And medieval times *were* sexist. No Buffys hanging on corners. We don't have any costumes—"

"I'll wear this." Kristin pulled a costume from the rack. "And I'll need a wooden stake." She looked thoughtful. "Guess you don't have a cross or some holy water."

No way was he putting a pointed object in her evil little hands. "Sorry, all out of religious symbols. Ditto for wooden stakes." What the hell was *that* costume all about? "You're going to wear a pair of baggy pants, an oversized shirt, and a long brown robe?" Not very sexy for someone who was looking for *sex*, hoping for *sex*, and dying to write a sensational story about *sex*. Yeah, so he was bitter.

"Mmm." She headed for one of the dressing cubicles. "I'm disguised as a boy because women were forbidden to be vampire slayers in medieval times."

Taurin tried to sound doubtful. Frustrated teeth-grinding wouldn't get him anywhere. "Not your usual fantasy. Besides, Conall always destroys the vampire."

"Not this time." Kristin's sensual mouth was set in a stubborn line. "Conall can get there in time to exclaim over the wonder of a mere *woman* taking out the undead."

He watched her disappear behind the cubicle's curtain before yanking his costume off the rack. Then with a muttered curse, he stepped into a cubicle.

Why the hell was he so mad? She could wear a sack for all he cared. He'd be naked enough for both of them. Stripping off his clothes, he pulled the cape around him. Then he paused.

No, he wouldn't let her make him completely crazy. Eric was right. What if someone other than Kristin got a glance at what *wasn't* under his cape? Picking up his jeans, he pulled out his cell phone and called Eric. When Eric answered, Taurin didn't give him time to talk.

"Don't ask questions. I need a swimsuit. Any swimsuit. And make it fast." As he whispered into the phone, Taurin looked out to make sure Kristin was still busy changing.

"Decided to hedge your bets?" Eric sounded amused. "Why not just keep your underwear on?"

Taurin let the silence pile up behind Eric's question. He could feel Eric processing the silence and then his expected hoot of laughter.

Taurin hoped Eric could feel the frost collecting on the other end of the line. "Hot handymen don't need underwear." He shut Eric off in mid-guffaw.

He listened to the sounds of Kristin sliding the curtain back from her cubicle. She paused outside his curtain.

"You ready yet?"

"No." He could hear her rooting through some of the props. "Go on out. Holgarth will get you started on the fantasy. I'll be along in a few minutes."

"Okay." There was an ominous clanking noise before she opened the door and left.

When Eric suddenly appeared in front of him, Taurin barely flinched. Preternatural speed was one of the perks of being a vampire. He'd never appreciated it more than he did now. "Let's have it." He held out his hand.

Eric gave him a small piece of metallic blue material sporting gold suns, moons, and stars. "Holgarth's. The best I could do on short notice."

Taurin stared at it. "*Holgarth* wears this?" He shut down all mental images. Nope, didn't want to go there *ever*.

"Yep." Eric was enjoying this way too much. "Hey, don't complain. This whole plan was your idea."

Taurin waited for Eric to leave, and then with a muttered curse, he pulled on the tiny blue stretchy abomination, all the while trying not to picture Holgarth leaping into the pool wearing only his blue wizard's hat and matching swimsuit.

Baring his fangs, Taurin pulled his cape closed and left the room in search of Kristin. She'd pay for this. Oh, yeah, she'd *really* pay.

He smiled.

CHAPTER ◆ TWO

"Madam, you will go directly to the dungeon. You will not pass Go, and you definitely will *not* collect two hundred dollars." Holgarth pursed his thin lips and pierced her with his beady-eyed glare. "And may I say that you have abysmal taste in costumes. Perhaps you intend to audition for *Monks Gone Wild*?"

Kristin narrowed her eyes to angry slits. "Whatever happened to 'the customer is always right'?"

Holgarth arched one supercilious brow. "Customers are rarely right. They need guidance. I'm positive that our handsome prince will have zero incentive to save your little behind—although one can't quite judge the scope of your derriere in that hideous outfit—when he has so many other beautifully garbed maidens from whom to choose."

"Handsome prince. Whoopee." Amazing. He'd reduced

her to a sulky ten-year-old with his formidable sarcasm. You had to respect that kind of power.

The wizard's harrumph expressed his supreme disapproval. "Most women are ecstatic at the chance to have a brave warrior engage an evil vampire in battle for their honor. And they welcome the handsome prince with the pitiful hope that he will bring them—dare I say it—ultimate bliss."

"Gag me. That is so pathetic." For just a teeny, tiny moment, the possibility of "ultimate bliss" with her hot handyman did skitter across her consciousness, but she whacked it with her mental broom before it could take her out of focus-on-the-job mode.

"I don't need a man to save me, and no way is anyone carrying me anywhere." She could picture the handsome prince grunting mightily as he tried to heave her into his arms. The visual made her smile. Okay, so she hadn't lost her sense of humor completely.

Holgarth didn't deign to argue as he eyed her weapon of choice. "My God, woman, what do you intend to do with *that*?"

"Slay the evil vampire myself." Kristin frowned at the huge sword. It was so heavy she had to drag it along the floor. She was counting on the adrenaline rush of battle to help her heft the dumb hunk of metal. "I think your warrior guy would have it easier if the castle stocked things like crosses, garlic, holy water, and wooden stakes."

"Where's the passion in a clove of garlic?" Holgarth looked down his long nose at her. "Medieval times were hardly romantic, although most women enjoy suspending their disbelief for a short time. But if you fancy yourself a warrior princess, I think we have an old Xena costume somewhere." His contemptuous sniff said that warrior princesses were so five minutes ago.

"The sword will have to go, though. We'll be lucky if you don't decapitate someone. Hopefully it won't be you. I do *not* want to defend the castle against a messy lawsuit. Do you think your family would be open to a discreet out-of-court settlement?" He seemed to brighten at the possibility of her decapitation without legal consequences.

Kristin closed her eyes for a moment to gather her wits, which seemed to have fled to places unknown. What was her problem? And why was she dressed in this ridiculous brown robe while she dragged a really big phallic symbol behind her? Jeez, she was here to find sex, and she didn't think she'd find much of it dressed like a frumpy paper sack. A scary truth hid just out of sight, but she didn't have time right now for deep introspection.

"Look, it's my fantasy, and if I want to wear this costume, I'll damn well wear it. The sword stays with me, unless you want to wrestle me for it." How did this place ever get any customers if they had to go through Mr. Snarky first? "And what if I don't feel like going to the dungeon?"

Holgarth sighed dramatically. "The fantasies are scheduled at half-hour intervals. The fantasy lasts twenty minutes, and the actors have ten minutes to prepare for the next one. I had no idea that you would *fling* yourself into my carefully planned schedule, but Taurin insists you must experience a fantasy right now. So in order to accommodate you 'right now,' *I* will choose your fantasy."

Kristin frowned. As much as she'd love to argue with him about that, she had to admit he had a point. "Fine, so where's the dungeon? Will Eric the Evil be there?"

Holgarth nodded as he pointed imperiously toward a darkened stairway on the other side of the great hall. "Go. The vampire awaits."

"Oh, stuff the melodrama." Not impressive as putdowns went, but she was too busy thinking about her confrontation with the vampire to worry about Holgarth. As she dragged her really big sword across the hall, people turned to stare. What? Hadn't they ever seen a female vampire slayer dressed like Friar Tuck before?

She peered down the stone stairway that spiraled into blackness. A few puny wall sconces barely made a dent in the darkness. Kristin swallowed hard. Okay, this wasn't real, so why the clammy hands and noisy gulps?

Time for some self-truth here. She was afraid. Oh, not of the dark, but of what waited in the darkness. *Sex.* It crouched at the bottom of the stairway, ready to pounce and tear away her protective layer of bravado. Sex was up close and personal, not something she could back away from and view objectively. She'd feel a lot braver facing werewolves in Minnesota.

Sure, she wanted a kinky sex story because it would sell like crazy, and because she really liked the *concept* of kinky sex. And yeah, she'd covered a few sex stories, but she'd always had someone else on the inside doing the grunt work. Had she phrased that wrong? Anyway, all she'd had to do was write the article. This was different. She didn't have a buffer zone this time.

So? The shocking truth washed over her and nearly took her under. She was a product of her repressed background. When in doubt, blame your parents.

She'd made love before, but she'd never been comfortable with it, had never been able to lose herself in the event. It was always like she was standing off to the side critiquing herself and her partner—she'd be doing the penguin waddle if she didn't hit the gym soon; he was making really funny noises; and had she paid her cable bill? All in all, making love had been just okay. If she couldn't turn off all her inner dialogue, she doubted she'd ever experience the ultimate *wow!* moment.

But hope sprang eternal and all that crap. She still held out hope for the man who could make her forget her cable bill while giving her an orgasm that would reduce her to tears of gratitude.

It wouldn't happen this week. She had to stay focused on her job. If the park was all about sex, and if she took her investigation to its logical conclusion, she wouldn't be making love. She'd be having sex with a stranger, one of women's top ten fantasies, according to research. It tempted at the same time it scared the hell out of her.

This was the start of a whole week of searching for sex around every corner while she wondered with heart-pounding uncertainty what she'd do if she found it.

Okay, now that she understood where she was coming from, she could concentrate on where she was going. Right now it was down these stairs.

Kristin crept downward, step by agonizing step, and

she'd swear the *kaboom*, *kaboom* of her heartbeat echoed off the stone walls like a demented kettledrum. The *clank, clank* of her sword as it hit each step added to the general din. She sure wasn't doing a good job of creeping up on Eric the Evil. Even as she crept, he was probably polishing his fangs.

Kristin took a deep breath. More oxygen would calm her heart into a false sense of security. She *could* walk to the bottom of this staircase. She *could* meet and defeat Eric the Evil. She *could* find out if he had sex on his mind. She could . . . She *could* run like hell back up the steps and face the patronizing sneer of the castle's wicked wizard.

Never. Besides, it was too late to run. She'd reached the bottom of the steps. She paused to take stock. There were several doors revealed by the one wall sconce's yellow glow. She supposed the dungeon's door was the big ugly one with a few tastefully arranged blood splatters. Ugh.

Personally, she had questions about the other doors. Storerooms? Labs where mad scientists carried out unspeakable experiments on armadillos? Kristin couldn't help it. She was drawn to the outrageous.

Dragging her attention back to the dungeon door, she sighed. No way could she put this off any longer. Kristen opened the door and stepped into the dungeon's dim interior.

He moved from the shadows, just a large dark shape until he stepped into the dim circle of light cast by one of the dungeon's four flickering candles. He used one hand to hold closed the folds of his long black cape while with his other he held a flap of the cape over most of his face.

Someone needed to give this guy a vampire fashion makeover. Her mole inside the San Antonio group had told her vampire wannabes dressed pretty much like everyone else. She would've checked it out herself, but the pics he'd sent her showed nothing but empty rooms. She'd meant to ask him about the pics, but he disappeared right after sending them. Weird.

Eric the Evil needed to trade in his cape for jeans and a T-shirt. She opened her mouth to tell him that, but swallowed hard instead.

Okay, so he had the whole dark, dank dungeon thing going on, and it was sort of creeping her out. Stone floor, stone walls, a variety of torture instruments, and a big black-caped guy standing in the middle of it all were enough to put a chill in the air. She shivered. Kudos to whoever was in charge of sets here.

"And what did Holgarth send me tonight?" His soft laughter sounded more sinister than amused. "I assume you're a choice morsel, but it's hard to tell with all the brown wrapping paper. Come to me so I can strip away all those layers and sample your life's essence."

"Choice morsel? You've gotta be kidding." She clenched both hands around the sword as she prepared to attempt to lift it, oh say, maybe five inches off the floor. "And let's do away with euphemisms. You want to suck my blood, vampire." Wait, he didn't sound like Eric, but his voice *was* familiar, even muffled by the cape.

Nina Bangs

His laughter was more sincere this time. "Lots of attitude. I like it. Any ideas about how you'll reach my neck with that sword? I won't have any trouble reaching yours." He stepped closer.

"Taurin?" She knew it was his voice, and yet it wasn't. His voice seemed deeper, with a disturbing note of compulsion in it. Compulsion? Okay, time for some brain defogging.

"Not at this moment in this place." He moved even closer, invading her space, blocking out the light, and filling her total field of vision with intimidating male.

She resisted the urge to back up and tried to immerse herself in the fantasy. "Come any closer, and I'll . . . cut you off at the ankles." Kristin sensed his smile behind his improvised mask.

"Can't lift that sword any higher, huh?"

"Stupid sword."

"I guess I could bend down, but I have a better idea." Taking that last step, he wrapped his arms around her and pulled her close. "Let's explore coexistence strategies."

Kristin noticed something right away. He had to let go of his cape in order to hold her. The cape gaped open. There was lots of bare vampire pressed against her.

She mentally stroked her chin. Ah, so the rumors of sex in the citadel were true. "Sex and the Citadel," a great title for her article.

Time for her to put her investigative skills to use. She wiggled her body against his to get a feel for the situation. Mmm, hard muscle beneath smooth skin. Too bad she couldn't ditch her dumb costume. It always paid to get close to your subject, the closer the better.

His body heat warmed her. Everywhere. Sweat pooled between her breasts and trickled a sensual path south where the action was sizzling. Her Center for Sexual Excitement had realized the potential for imminent erotic diversion and kicked into high gear. All that tactile stimulation along with the heavy feeling building low in her belly made her drop her useless sword so she could reach for her robe.

As he released her, she glanced at his face. And froze.

Whoever did the makeup here was a pro. Sure the dungeon was dark, but she was close enough to spot a phony vampire face. Taurin's face looked as real as her own. Well, maybe not quite as *human* as her own. He was vampire. His eyes were larger and sort of elongated. And they were the blackest eyes she'd ever seen. But it was his mouth that riveted her. His lips were fuller, more sensual, *tempting*.

He smiled, a wicked lifting of his lips that exposed gleaming fangs. Kristin shuddered. At least she knew why his mouth looked so sexy. He was covering up some serious dental hardware.

She was conflicted. On one hand, even in vampire form he was so hot she expected the air around him to ignite. On the other hand, those were some heavy-duty canines. And she'd been right, they were white and shiny— evidence that he did a lot of polishing.

"Come to me, Kristin." His low, husky murmur promised she wouldn't be sorry.

Kristin took a deep breath. Reality-check time. This was just a fantasy. His fangs were fake. Taurin wasn't a vampire; he was just a sexy guy. And she'd always known she'd have to make sacrifices for her job.

She slipped out of her robe and flung it away from her.

In the name of investigative reporting, she'd offer herself up on the altar of doing-whatever-it-takes. She'd force herself to run her hands over that incredible chest, touch his male nipples with her tongue, and put her mouth wherever her lips felt the need to wander.

She unbuttoned her shirt and let it slide to the floor.

No matter how grueling the investigation process was, she'd carry on until she had every last sordid detail. It would be tough work exploring all those out-of-the-way spots on his muscular body. But hey, her readers would want to know the texture and the exact degree of firmness of his magnificent butt cheeks.

She reached for her pants' button.

No one could say she didn't throw herself into her work. Oh, the sacrifices she made for the sake of her art. She paused with her fingers still on the button. Oh, the lies she told. Who was she trying to kid? What she wanted to do with Taurin would never appear in print.

Kristin let her fingers linger on the button a little longer as she slid her gaze the length of his body. Hmm. "Tell me you're not wearing a blue metallic swimsuit with gold suns, moons, and stars."

"Holgarth's. It was either this or nothing at all."

He glanced away and she would've sworn he looked embarrassed. This touch of human weakness made her feel all soft and mushy inside. "Personally, I would've come down on the side of nothing."

"Hmmph. A real man wouldn't stand around talking everything to death. When are you gonna get to the good stuff? I don't have all night." The grouchy male voice came from one of the darkened corners.

Kristin gasped and quickly bent down to retrieve her shirt. Taurin cursed as he spun toward the voice. How the hell had someone gotten in without him knowing?

"Jeez, close the damn cape, man. Lookin' at a mostly naked vampire gives me hives." The fluffy white Persian cat stepped from the shadows and stared up at Taurin from big round blue eyes.

"Who're you?" Taurin hoped he scared the crap out of the cat. He bared his fangs to emphasize how pissed he was. A few more minutes and Kristin would've been naked in his arms. He'd wanted that. *Really* wanted it.

"That cat talked to you." Kristin stood clutching her shirt, eyes wide with shock.

"Yeah, but he won't be talking much longer, because I'm kicking his furry ass out of here." Taurin glared at the cat.

The cat ignored Taurin's threat in favor of staring at Kristin. "Lookin' good, babe. If I were in my human form, the action would've started long ago."

"It's talking to *me* now." Kristin seemed stuck on that one thought.

Taurin forced himself to calm down. Heaving a shape-shifter from the dungeon might involve a battle, which would upset Kristin even more than she was now. "You haven't answered my question."

"I'm S.O.B., and you bloodsuckers are a bunch of wusses. I'm a real man. I control the remote, and I leave the toilet seat up if I damn well feel like it. Women love a man who takes charge and doesn't put up with crap from anyone." He seemed to puff up right before Taurin's eyes. "Women need a strong man to tell them what to do."

"Whoa, there, kitty." Kristin might be in shock over a talking cat, but she was still able to react to the red flag S.O.B. unwisely waved in her face. "You might be all cute and fluffy, but beneath all that fur beats the heart of a sexist jerk."

She cast Taurin a panicked glance. "Tell me I'm not arguing with a cat."

"S.O.B.? Is that a character judgment?" Taurin took a step toward the cat.

The cat ignored him. From the glitter in his eyes, Taurin figured he was totally pissed.

"Don't call me cute and fluffy, woman. I'm a mean fighting machine. My enemies run screaming when they see me coming. I eat chunks of concrete for lunch. I—"

Kristin's eyes still looked glazed, but her fighting spirit seemed in great shape. "You're cute and fluffy. Deal with it."

Taurin recognized the exact moment her nose for a sensational story began to twitch. "So what's the trick? Is the kitty wired and someone upstairs is spouting this stuff? If so, you really need a new script writer." She stared at Taurin. "Tell me we're dealing with a wired kitty."

What could he say to reassure her? Nothing. So he talked to the cat instead. "What're you doing here?"

The cat whipped its tail back and forth, still ticked at Kristin. "I was just hanging, so I thought I'd kill time watching you guys. I'd have more fun watching mold grow."

Kristin slipped into her shirt and crouched down in front of the cat. She ran her hands over its body looking for the wire.

"Won't find anything, but don't let that stop you."

Kristin paled as she stood and turned to Taurin. "Nothing. What's going on?"

Taurin raked his fingers through his hair. Okay, one thing at a time. "Let me rephrase my question. Why the hell are you in the castle?"

"Oh, that. I'm a messenger of Bast, Egyptian cat goddess of all things important, according to her. A while ago Bast sent another messenger, Asima, to the castle. Asima hasn't reported in lately, so the goddess sent me to check on things. Seen this Asima chick around anywhere?"

Kristin put her hand over her mouth. Probably trying to muffle a scream.

"I might've. What's your whole name? I won't call you S.O.B., even if it fits." Taurin kept an eye on Kristin. He hoped she wouldn't have hysterics or race screaming up the stairs.

The cat stared at him resentfully. He mumbled a name.

"Again. Didn't quite catch that name." Taurin bared his fangs to hint he was losing patience.

"Oh, hell. It's Saffron." He hissed the name.

"That's the *S*. How about the *O* and *B*?" Taurin relaxed a little as Kristin dropped her hand from her mouth and seemed to be listening to the cat.

"My name's Saffron Oregano Basil." He growled low in his throat. "You laugh, you're dead."

It was tough. Taurin wanted to laugh. Kristin just stared at Saffron with wide, unblinking eyes.

"Okay, Saffron, you can leave now." He wanted to be alone with Kristin. Not that he had any hope of picking up where they'd left off.

"No." Kristin's voice was a little quivery, but sounded determined. "Who gave you that name? What are you? And can I have an exclusive on your story?"

She glanced at Taurin. "I'm still in denial here, but just in case this guy's for real, I want an interview."

Damn. He'd forgotten what she was. She recognized a sensational story when she saw it. The scariest part? If she accepted the shape-shifter as real, she might begin wondering about the reality of other nonhuman entities. He couldn't let that happen.

"Don't waste your time. He's a fake. We have a remote hookup that makes it sound like he's talking." Was that possible? He hadn't a clue. "He's, umm, Snowflake, my cat." Taurin glared at Saffron, daring him to deny it.

Saffron wasn't having any part of it. "Snowflake? What the hell kind of name is that? It's as bad as Saffron."

He shifted his attention back to Kristin. "I'm real. Don't doubt it. The deal is that goddesses are touchy. See, I made the mistake of telling someone I'd rather serve Sekhmet, the lion goddess of war and destruction. That's a real man's goddess. Major mistake. Bast heard me. She's Sekhmet's sister, and they have this whole sisterly competition thing going on. Bast got pissed and gave me this form. All her messengers take cat form, but hey, she could've made me a big old alley cat. I would've been down with that."

"And the name. Tell me about the name." Kristin's eyes glowed with journalistic fervor.

Taurin wished she'd look at him like that. Fat chance after this. She'd run back to her room so she could load all her ammunition onto her laptop. Bummer.

Saffron did a cat shrug. "Bast was in her herb garden phase when she named me. The bit . . . um, goddess, knew I'd hate it. At least S.O.B. is an in-your-face name." He turned to look at the door. "I sense another messenger of Bast close by. Must be Asima. Talk to you guys later." And he was gone.

Much later, Taurin hoped. He glanced at his watch. Their fantasy time was almost up. Holgarth would be nagging Conall to go down and save the "fair maiden" so he could keep his schedule rolling right along. Hah! She needed saving like a tigress needed saving.

"Look, the fantasy is pretty much blown, so why

don't I make it up to you by taking you to one of the other fantasies in the park tomorrow night?" He had to get out of here, because he couldn't change back to human form while she was watching.

Her steady stare told him a lot was going on in that beautiful head. All bad news for him. "You're not surprised, are you? It's like you deal with talking cats every day. Why is that?"

Because Asima is underfoot all the time, and she never shuts up. Taurin studied Kristin's expression. She bought Saffron's story. Even so, he had to stick with his take on the whole thing or risk opening a door he couldn't close again. "He startled me, but like I said, he's a fake. They just started using him this week. And my reaction was part of the fantasy. Anyway, I'm a guy, and it's a guy thing to make believe that nothing shocks us. Like if Bigfoot walked in front of a bunch of guys, they'd just wave and say, 'What's happening, dude?'" Did any of that make sense? Not too much.

"Yeah, like I believe that." But she did reward his effort with a tiny smile. Holding his gaze, she drew close. "Great makeup."

And before he could back away from her, she reached up and traced the shape of his eye with the tip of her index finger. Alarm flared in her eyes as she jerked her hand away from his face. Uh-oh.

"I've gotta go now. Uh, I have to write down my thoughts while everything is still fresh in my mind." She turned without waiting for his reply.

Taurin watched her grab her robe from where it was

draped over the fake iron maiden and scurry up the steps. Well, hell. Looked like he had a situation here. He followed her more slowly as he returned to human form.

Sure, he could ask Eric to try to erase the event from her memory, but something in him didn't want to do that. Maybe Saffron had a point. Asking another man to fix the mess he'd created made him feel weak. Yeah, it was probably a guy thing. And no, he didn't ask for directions, either.

A puzzled Eric met him at the top of the steps. "What happened? Kristin just tore past me like she'd seen a ghost."

"No ghost, just a friend of Asima's."

"Oh, shit."

"In cat form."

"Oh, shit."

"He talked to her."

"Oh, shit."

"Yeah." He walked away from Eric. Wouldn't do any good to mention that Kristin had also traced around his eyes. From the look on her face, she'd realized he wasn't wearing makeup or a mask.

So what was he going to do? Maybe he'd find Saffron and rip off his fuzzy head.

CHAPTER ◆ THREE

Kristin sat on the couch, staring at her laptop while she tried to make sense of what she'd just written. She'd wanted to get it all down while everything was fresh in her mind. Maybe freshness wasn't a good thing. Maybe this story needed to age a little. It was a tangle of sex, shape-shifters, and vampires. No one would believe her. She didn't believe herself.

Okay, look at the facts. Taurin had shown up wearing just a swimsuit and a cape. Hello? Can we say dressed for an episode of *Desire in the Dungeon*? So, yeah, the castle seemed to be working on a sexual theme.

Next came Saffron. Maybe the castle did have some really high-tech special effects, but until she had proof of that, she was taking the cat at face value.

Finally, the part that bothered her the most. When she'd traced Taurin's eyes, she'd found no evidence of a mask or makeup. No, she wasn't ready to accept *that* reality yet. She'd sleep on it, and take a second look at the evidence tomorrow.

Shutting down her laptop, she pulled on her nightshirt and climbed into bed. She tried to relax by rereading some of the info she'd gathered about the park. Every attempt she'd made to track down the owner of Live the Fantasy had ended with a door slammed in her face. Curious. Very curious.

She read until her lids started to droop. But just as she reached for the bedside lamp, the door swung open.

What the . . . ? She'd locked that door. Frantically, she fumbled for the phone to call for help.

"Oh, for crying out loud, put the phone down. It's just me."

Kristin dropped the receiver from nerveless fingers as she stared at the blue point Siamese cat that padded across the room and then leaped onto the foot of her bed. She tried to force words past the boulder lodged in her throat. "Me?" *And why am I hearing you in my head?*

Even with limited kitty facial muscles, the cat managed to look annoyed. *"I'm Asima, messenger of Bast. I realize I'm not the first messenger of Bast you've met tonight, but I assure you I'm much more civilized than that big white booby you met earlier. I'd never inject myself into a sensual moment between two people."* The cat sat and began to wash its face with one elegant paw. *"Please close your mouth, you look silly."* She paused in her grooming to offer Kristin a pointed stare. *"And I'm speaking in your head because I'm discreet, as opposed to Saffron, who never understood the whole keeping-our-existence-secret concept."*

Kristin knew Asima expected a comment, but how could she think when her brain was filled with white noise? Well, maybe white noise along with an occasional silent shriek. Wait, had Asima read her mind? Unlikely. Right now her mind was putting out a series of random scribbles.

"You're probably wondering why I chose to use some of my incredibly valuable time visiting with you." Asima didn't need Kristin's input. She was capable of carrying on a semi-intelligent conversation with herself. *"I thought I'd better attempt some damage control. Eric could probably wipe your memory clean, but he really doesn't like to do that if it's not necessary. And you look like a reasonable woman."*

"Wipe my memory clean?" The cat was talking in her head. In. Her. *Head.*

"Mmm. I'm sure if you agree not to say anything about the beings who live in the castle, Eric won't have to use his power." Finished with her face, Asima glanced at Kristin's closet. *"Do you mind if I take a peek at your clothes? You can tell a lot about a person by what they wear."*

"Beings?" Kristin was falling behind in this conversation.

"Oops." Asima put her paw over her little cat mouth. *"A mere slip of the tongue. Forget it."* But the sly gleam in her blue eyes said she definitely didn't want Kristin to forget it. *"So can I look at your clothes?"*

"Uh-huh." Kristin couldn't force any other words past her frozen lips.

Numb with shock, she watched Asima stare at her closet door. The door swung open and Asima disappeared inside. A few minutes later she emerged dragging a silky blue scarf behind her.

"Would you mind if I borrowed this until tomorrow? I'm meeting Saffron for dinner, and this will set off my eyes perfectly." Without waiting for Kristin's permission, she padded to the door trailing the scarf behind her. *"What wonderfully classic taste you have in clothes. Your casual things are stylish without being slutty, and I love the dresses you brought. If I were in my human form, I'd ask to borrow the white one."*

A human form was good. Kristin would gladly sacrifice her white dress if it meant she could keep her sanity, because this whole scene was too bizarre to be real.

"I'll get this back to you tomorrow." Asima dragged the scarf to the door that still stood open. She paused before leaving. *"Give Taurin a chance. He's a nice guy who's had some bad breaks. Everyone needs something good to happen to them at least once every few centuries."*

Every few centuries? While Kristin stared blankly, Asima padded into the hallway, her waving tail a satisfied question mark above her back. The door closed with a quiet *click*.

Ohmigod, ohmigod! Clambering from the bed, Kristin rushed to the door, stubbing her toe on a chair along the way. Ow! Definitely awake. She was panting by the time she reached the door. Hyperventilating wouldn't help anything.

She checked to make sure the door was locked and then slid the chain across it.

Why was she doing this? Locks wouldn't keep Asima out. And what other kinds of "beings" roamed the dark halls of the castle? Beings that would think of a lock as a minor annoyance.

Kristin stumbled back to her bed, fell onto it, and pulled the covers over her head. She lay there curled into a fetal position with her teeth chattering. Just great. The biggest story of her freaking career, and she was never coming out from under these covers.

The first thing Kristin saw when she woke was the clock. Three o'clock. She groaned. She must've been exhausted to sleep half the afternoon away.

Then she remembered—Saffron, Taurin, Asima, and Eric who could take away her memory if she proved not to be a "reasonable" woman. If she ran downstairs right now and found Eric, would he take his little pink eraser to her memory of last night?

A loud pounding on her door distracted her from thoughts of Eric and erasers. The knocking was what must've awakened her. Who was on the other side? One of the castle's many "beings"? Taurin? She ignored her sudden spurt of excitement. No chance. If he was what she suspected—please, please don't let him be *that*—he wouldn't rise until dark.

Kristin mentally pushed aside the panicked shouts of her common sense urging her to pack her bags and get her tail out of town. She'd waited her whole career for a story like this. It had everything—sex, nonhuman entities, and a compelling setting.

She crawled out of bed, pulled on her robe, and walked to the door. Yes, nonhuman entities. Somewhere during the sleepless early hours of the morning—it'd been seven the last time she'd looked at her clock—she'd accepted the reality of what she'd experienced. Except for Taurin. Now she had to deal with it.

Kristin put her ear to the door. "Who's there?" At least she knew it wasn't Asima. Asima didn't knock.

"Banan." Sexy male voice.

"Are you a vampire?"

Long pause. "No."

"How about a cat?"

"No." Sounded insulted.

"Do you have all your clothes on?"

A longer pause. "If that's what you want."

With a huff of impatience, Kristin pulled open her door.

After meeting Taurin and Eric, she wasn't surprised to see another great-looking guy, but Banan was something more. He was scary. That, of course, lowered his rating on her personal hot-hunk scale.

"I don't see a pot of fresh-brewed coffee in your hand, so I assume you have the wrong room."

As tall as Taurin and Eric, he wore his khaki shorts and sleeveless T-shirt well. They showcased his broad shoulders and strong arms and legs. He was all lean, sculpted muscle.

"Oh, I have the right room, Kristin." He smiled.

Uh-oh. Unease danced along her nerves. What was it about this guy? For a start, he had long pale hair that almost reached his butt. It should've looked lank and limp. It should've made him look sort of feminine. It should've made him look washed-out. It did none of the above. It just made him look scary. And sexy. Couldn't forget sexy. His hair seemed to hold all the colors of the universe in each strand, and she had the feeling she would see them all if only she could catch him in the right light.

He had the prerequisite sensual mouth that all hot guys needed in order to qualify, but his eyes . . . They were so dark she couldn't see his pupils. And maybe her imagination was still overstimulated from last night, but Kristin could swear she was looking into the eyes of a predator.

She rubbed the back of her hand across her forehead in the hope that the gesture would clear her thoughts. Banan was just a guy with an unusual hair and eye combination. Spectacular, but nothing to send her into full retreat. Last night was messing with her mind.

"And you're here why?" Kristin met his gaze.

He shrugged. "For whatever you want. We could take in a few of the fantasies in the park or go down to the beach. Get some sun. Play in the surf." His lips lifted in another smile, exposing white teeth that somehow looked menacing.

Oh, let it go, Hughes. He had great-looking teeth, *normal*-looking teeth. Taurin was the one with the chilling dental work.

"Playing in the surf sounds great, but ask me again tomorrow. I overslept today. Gotta get moving on my story. I'll stay in the castle for a few hours and interview people, try to get a feel for the place." A lie. She wanted to be around when Taurin showed up. *Before* sunset. She hoped. "By the way, who sent you?"

Banan studied her with those dark eyes. "Holgarth. Taurin's showing you around at night, but he's . . . busy during the day. I'm not." He shrugged. "So here I am."

"Taurin's showing me around? Who made that official?" There was something not quite right about this whole deal, beyond the talking cats and vampire thing.

"Holgarth. He said if you're doing a story about the park, you need someone to show you around." He shrugged. "If you change your mind, I'll be hanging down at the beach until dark." He nodded in the direction of Seawall Boulevard, which separated the Castle of Dark Dreams from the Gulf.

Kristin watched him walk away. Strange man. If she was serious about searching for sex, she should try to hook up with him and see where he led her.

Not interested. The only one in the castle she wanted to hook up with was Taurin. A surprising revelation considering everything that had happened last night. He'd have a lot of explaining to do when she saw him, but she was open to being convinced that last night wasn't what it had seemed.

Kristin turned from the door. She wanted coffee, a shower, and some exciting gossip about hot sex in ye olde castle. Surely there was one employee who worked here willing to spill his or her guts for instant fame and maybe a small bribe.

Or not. Hours later, she'd grilled everyone who'd stand still long enough to listen to her broad hints about how grateful she'd be to anyone willing to point her in the direction of sex and sin. Sex and sin score? Zero. Dumb people. Kristin gave up for the day.

All she'd gotten for her trouble were some strange looks, a few giggles, and one pamphlet inviting her to visit the Church of Eternal Salvation.

Even more troubling was the fact that late afternoon was fading into dusk and Taurin was nowhere in sight. She was deep into denial. He'd probably been up for hours. Just because she hadn't seen him didn't mean he wasn't doing his handyman thing somewhere in the castle. Or maybe it was his day off, and he'd stayed in his room to catch *Oprah* or *Dr. Phil*. Yeah, like she believed that.

Finally, she couldn't stand it anymore. Her nerves were shredded. She'd walk on the beach to calm herself down, maybe run into Banan. He might answer a few questions if she was persistent enough. After all, the early mosquito got the blood. Ugh, blood. Nope, wouldn't think about Taurin. Not giving herself time for second thoughts, she headed for the door.

"He'll be down soon." The deep masculine voice spun her around. The man was big, muscular, and smiling. "Sorry to scare you. I'm Conall, Eric's brother. Asima pointed you out. I figured you were waiting for Taurin."

Okay, going all defensive here. "Uh-uh, not me. I was . . . just looking for people to interview for my story. In fact, I have an appointment with Banan right now. I'm meeting him on the beach." She offered him a plastic smile.

Conall frowned. "Banan? Maybe you should wait until Taurin gets here. He can go with you."

Now see, he'd gone and said the wrong thing. "I can walk to the beach all by myself. I don't need anyone tagging along. It was great meeting you." Kristin knew he was still watching her as she escaped through the door.

It only took a few minutes to cross Seawall Boulevard and go down the steps to the beach. With darkness falling quickly, the beach had emptied out. Looking around, she spotted Banan sitting on the sand staring at the Gulf. Kristin walked over and sat down beside him.

"How's it going?" She joined him in staring at the water.

"Decided to come after all?" He turned and smiled at her.

Nightfall made him look even more spectacular. Why wasn't she tempted? Probably because he was still a scary guy. "Yeah, I needed to get out of the castle. Besides, there was always the chance that I could pump some info about the castle out of you."

His smile never dimmed. "Wouldn't count on it. Want to go for a swim?"

"Isn't it a little late for that? No lifeguards around." She didn't miss the eagerness in his voice. "You must like the water a lot to sit out here all afternoon."

"I love the seas. I have to be near them." His voice had taken on a hypnotic singsong cadence. "Come with me and play in the water."

"Uh, I don't think so, but don't let me stop you. I'll just sit here and watch." This guy was seriously strange.

He stood and glanced around at the empty beach. Kristin followed his gaze. Hmm. It was almost completely dark and they had the beach all to themselves. A prickle of unease suggested that maybe she should go back to the castle, that being here alone with a man—a man her instincts were telling her felt wrong—wasn't too smart.

But she had a story to write, and he hadn't said or done one threatening thing. This time she'd ignore her instincts.

She rethought that decision as he stripped off his shorts and T-shirt. No swimsuit underneath. Yikes.

The grin he turned on her was almost boyish. "I swim nude. I get off on the feel of freedom with nothing between me and the water."

"Uh, good." Kristin's gaze skittered away from him. Great. She was here to write a story about sex, but when she found it, she did a dumb-virgin act. *Get over it.* She looked. Very nice.

"Do me a favor? Wade into the surf. You don't have to go in past your thighs, but you can hand my shorts to me when I come out." He laughed. And for the first time she didn't feel the danger. "I don't want to be stuck out there if a bunch of people show up."

Kristin didn't think a bunch of people would show up in the pitch dark. Sure there was some moonlight, but not much. She saw his point, though. A cop might come down to the beach to see what was going on. Banan wouldn't want to chance an indecent exposure charge.

Besides, July in Galveston was damn hot, and night

didn't cool things down much. The wind was blowing, but it just pushed the hot air around. The water would feel good. "Okay, but don't go out too far. I don't do water rescues."

He handed his shorts to her, and she followed him down to the waterline. As he raced into the water, she admired the rear view. Trophy-quality butt.

Banan had already disappeared into the surf by the time she waded out to where the water lapped at the hem of her shorts. Warm water. So much for heat relief. The waves were low and choppy, but she wasn't in any danger of being knocked off her feet.

As she stood waiting for Banan to emerge, her thoughts wandered to Taurin. Would he show up at her door and wonder where she'd gone? Kristin sure hoped so. He'd promised her another fantasy to make up for last night. Funny, but the shiver that thought brought had nothing to do with fear and everything to do with awareness.

Besides, the whole vampire thing from last night seemed sort of silly now. He'd probably been wearing a pliable mask and she'd been too overwhelmed by Saffron to recognize it. He'd explain everything when she saw him again.

Where the heck was Banan? She hadn't seen him surface. Kristin edged out farther into the surf until she was up to her waist in the water. Worry tugged at her. She hadn't grown up around water, but she'd made up for that lack when she went to college in California. She knew the danger of rip currents.

As if on cue, a choppy wave broke over her and she felt the inexorable pull as the current dragged her out. Dammit, she should've paid closer attention. She should've recognized the warning signs. Kristin was a strong swimmer, and she knew how to escape a riptide. She let it take her and then began swimming parallel to the shore with the current. Had it gotten Banan?

Oh, God. Panic touched her. What if she'd lost him? Kristin raised her head to look around. Nothing but dark water. No, there was something.

A fin. Primal fear touched her, and she tried to swim faster. She almost cried with relief when she finally fought free of the current. Her breaths came in harsh gasps as she swam toward the shore. Suddenly, something brushed against her leg. Something huge. And she knew. Opening her mouth, she screamed.

The shark broke the surface right in front of her. Fear leached the strength from her, and for a moment she floundered in the water. *A great white.* In her mind, the theme from *Jaws* played counterpoint to the staccato beat of her heart.

Survival instincts kicked in as she remembered something from a TV program. Gathering all her strength, she punched the shark in the nose with every ounce of terror-driven power she could muster.

And the shark retreated. She couldn't believe it. But she wasn't going to hang around to revel in her success. She was doing a credible imitation of a windmill as she made for shore.

"Hang on! I'm coming." Taurin?

She blinked the water from her eyes and saw him fling himself down the steps of the seawall and onto the beach. As if in slow motion, she watched him scoop his

cell phone from his pocket and drop it onto the sand.
Then . . . Then he was beside her in the water. What
the . . . ? She blinked some more. He was wearing his
vampire face. Oh, crap.

"Relax. I have you." He wrapped his arms around
her, and before she even had a chance to gasp for air,
they were back on the beach. "Did he hurt you?"

The hell with the shark. Kristin started to reach toward his face, but before she could touch him, he became human again. No special effects, no trick of the
light. Taurin was a freaking vampire.

"Did he hurt you?" He grabbed her shoulders and
gave her a little shake.

Like that was going to make her better if she *was* hurt.
"No." She stared and stared and no matter how hard she
tried, she couldn't blink. "A vampire. Talking cats.
Where's the rabbit hole?" She glanced vaguely around.
"Has to be a rabbit hole around here somewhere. Where'd
you put the rabbit hole?" She was babbling, not a good
sign.

Taurin dropped his hands from her and raked his fingers through his wet hair. "This wasn't supposed to happen."

"No kidding." Kristin felt a little woozy. But she'd
be okay. She'd never fainted. She could take this. She
finally blinked. There was something important that she
knew she had to remember, something really important.
Impatiently, she pushed at the mental fog messing with
her thoughts.

"Why the hell did you go in the water anyway? Do you see a lifeguard anywhere?"

Kristin closed her eyes in an attempt to control a little spurt of dizziness. A second later they popped open. She'd remembered. "Ohmigod! I forgot. Banan is out there. We have to save him."

Taurin stared at something behind her. "No, we don't."

She turned. Banan was striding naked toward them. He looked steamed.

"Why'd you punch me in the nose when I was trying to save you? I bet you lost my shorts." He looked around. "Yep. They're gone. You'll have to go back to the castle and get me a new pair."

Kristin stared at his bloody nose. Her brain wasn't working at full force because her thoughts felt like they were slogging through knee-deep mud. "Why did I punch you in the nose?"

Nose. Punch. Shark. Naked guy coming out of water. Shark? Banan was a . . .

Kristin fainted.

CHAPTER ◆ FOUR

"Oh, shit." Taurin caught Kristin as she toppled, and eased her onto the sand. "Why'd you have to scare her like that?" He glared at Banan.

"Me?" The wereshark looked aggrieved. "I was trying to save her cute little butt. You're the one who charged into the water in full vampire mode. Using your preternatural speed to pop up next to her didn't help, either."

"Just remember, her cute little butt isn't yours." What was that about? He didn't remember signing ownership papers on any part of Kristin Hughes. All he cared about was watching that cute little butt wave good-bye as she left *without* a story.

Taurin retrieved his cell phone from the sand where he'd dropped it and then lifted her into his arms. He started toward the steps.

"Hey, what about my clothes?" Banan had retrieved his T-shirt and was wiping the blood from his nose.

Taurin considered leaving the shark bare-assed on the beach. The thought brightened his night. And he'd be damned if he'd let Banan play out any sexual fantasies with her like they'd originally planned.

So why the change in plans? Why all the negativity aimed at Banan? After all, the guy hadn't done anything to him. It was one of life's mysteries he'd explore later.

Setting Kristin down gently, he handed his phone to Banan and waited while the shark explained his situation to Holgarth. Taurin grinned. Knowing the power of the wizard's poison tongue, he'd guess Banan wasn't getting off easy.

By the time Banan gave back the cell phone, he was scowling. "If he has a brain under that pointed hat, Holgarth will never go into the water again." The shark's expression said he'd love to catch the wizard in *his* world.

Taurin forgot about Banan as Kristin stirred. She blinked and stared up at him. Then she stared at Banan.

"What happened?" She frowned.

"You checked out for a few minutes." Taurin watched her warily.

"I never faint."

Taurin saw the exact moment she remembered the sequence of definitely not-quite-normal events that had led to her "checking out." He expected her to scramble to her feet and make a break for the castle. She didn't.

"Sorry I dropped your shorts in the water. I owe you a new pair." As she stared at Banan, her expression turned calculating. "Maybe we should meet for lunch tomorrow. You could tell me how you change and—"

"He'll be busy tomorrow." Taurin scooped her off the sand, ignoring her startled squeak. "He has to spend the afternoon scaring the crap out of the tourists. Gives them something to tell friends about when they get home."

She glared up at him. "I can walk. Put. Me. Down."

"You'll run away."

"I know you're a vampire. I know I should run. But self-preservation takes a backseat to a sensational story."

He jogged across Seawall Boulevard with her in his arms.

"Oh, come on, you'll embarrass me if you carry me into the castle." She wiggled around in a vain attempt to free herself.

He hissed at her and, surprised, she shut up. "I'm not taking you into the castle. I'm taking you to my car, and then we're going to a place where we can talk without any damn cats interrupting us."

Before she could open her mouth to object, he set her down beside his car and unlocked the doors. "I won't bite you. You're booked for the week, and I never bite guests. But once the week is up, hey, all bets are off."

He jerked the car door open and glared at her. "You can walk away from me now, but I guarantee if you do you'll never get a story from this park."

Obviously the threat of losing her precious story did the trick. Without a word, she dropped into the passenger seat. Good thing it was so hot, because she was still soaking wet.

She remained silent until he pulled into the driveway of the beach house. "Yours?"

Okay, one word was a start. "No. It belongs to the castle. Any of us who feel the need for some downtime can come here to stay for a few days. Deimos—you haven't met him yet—is planning a midnight beach party here next Monday. You're invited."

He could slip into her mind, but not without her feeling him. Besides, he didn't need to. She figured the invite meant she'd still be alive for the party. The big, bad vampire wouldn't rip out her throat, suck her dry, and then leave her empty husk on the beach.

Taurin led the way around the side of the darkened house to the empty beach behind it. He found a spot well away from the water, yanked off his T-shirt, and spread it on the sand. "Sit."

"Thanks." She sat on his shirt before trying to finger-comb her hair. Then she lifted her face to the breeze. "That feels good."

Taurin sat beside her. Where to start? May as well get straight to the point. "You can't write about what you saw last night and tonight. No one will believe you. And you won't have any proof."

He could tell she was turning possibilities over in her mind. "You're right about no one believing me. That's not a problem, though. No one believed my story about werewolves in Minnesota, either, but lots of people tramped through the forests looking for them anyway." She didn't sound particularly discouraged. "Of course, I'd have to dodge Eric with his little pink mind-eraser. Even if I wrote the story, I couldn't defend it if I didn't remember what happened."

"Mind eraser? Who told you about Eric's power?"

"Asima. She thought I'd be comforted knowing that Eric wouldn't take away my memories if I acted like a reasonable woman."

Hah! Reasonable wasn't part of Kristin's vocabulary. And Asima stuck her snooty cat nose into everyone's business. She was an equal opportunity pest. "I'll make a deal with you. You'll get that sex story you want if you agree to forget about the paranormal stuff you've seen." He watched her wiggle her bottom into a more comfortable position. Her hair lay damp across her shoulders, and the tempting lines of her body stirred him in a way he didn't want to be stirred. Fine, so he wanted to be stirred, but not by her.

She turned to stare at him. "How'd you know about the sex story?" Then suspicion dawned in her eyes. "You read my mind, didn't you?"

He tried to smooth the tension from his smile. "Nope, can't do that. Only a few of the very old vampires, like Eric, have that power. Sorry. Another soulless bloodsucker myth goes down in flames."

She narrowed her gaze on him. "You're right, it wasn't you. You came to my room already dressed as a sexy handyman, so someone else knew about my story and decided to give me what I wanted. I wonder why?"

Uh-oh. He could almost hear her mental footsteps as she circled the question, studying it from every angle. Then the footsteps stopped.

Her smile was sweet and so wicked it shriveled his . . .

heart. "Gotcha! Whoever is at the top of this conspiracy ladder somehow knew I was coming to the castle looking for a kinky sex story. They decided to give it to me so I'd focus on the sex and not notice all the interesting 'beings' living here. But you, Saffron, Asima, and Banan blew it."

Slow and calm. Losing his temper wouldn't help the cause. He shrugged. "It doesn't matter now. What matters is your decision. What'll it be: authentic tales of hot sex from an actual witness—who, by the way, is Italian and therefore appreciates all things sensual—or unsubstantiated claims of nonhuman entity sightings? People will read both articles, but one of them pays a lot higher dividends."

She was thinking about her choices way too long. He was insulted. Her week's tour through Live the Fantasy with him would be a never-to-be-forgotten experience. Six hundred years of learning what women wanted guaranteed that.

He pushed aside the uncomfortable feeling that he was pimping himself out with this deal. It wasn't like he'd be having sex with her at every attraction in the park. He'd just be making up erotic stories about things that had never happened there. If he could preserve the Castle of Dark Dreams as a place where all his friends were safe, then it was worth it.

The tiny part of his brain dedicated to truth was laughing its ass off. Like it would be such a great sacrifice if he had to make love with Kristin. Uh-huh, right.

Kristin studied him as she tried to figure out how she could have both stories. Fact: Eric could take away her memory of everything that happened here. But if she made note of this possibility as soon as she got back to her room along with info about what had happened so far and e-mailed it to Connie, her best friend, then she could have her cake and eat it, too, so to speak.

And Taurin was a triple-layered Italian-cream cake. "You have a deal. I get info on all the sexual events you've witnessed, and I keep my mouth shut about all the paranormal stuff."

Sure, she felt a little guilty about lying, but she couldn't pass up a chance at the biggest story of her life. She'd salve her conscience by sharing her profits with Taurin. And in the end, her story would be great for Live the Fantasy's business. They'd rake in a fortune when people swarmed the place.

"Uh, just to satisfy my curiosity, why don't you want anyone to know you guys exist?" They'd be superstars. Larry King and Bill O'Reilly would fight for the right to interview them. David Letterman and Jay Leno would joke about them. Couldn't get bigger than that.

"Once humans know we exist, there'll be a certain segment who'll want to destroy us. Humans have a history of killing what they don't understand, either on religious grounds, or out of fear, or just for the hell of it. If you wrote that story and convinced enough people it was true, then lots of them would come sniffing around. All nonhumans would have to leave the castle, because we couldn't take the chance that one of the humans might get lucky."

Okay, now she felt really guilty. Unbidden, thoughts of her San Antonio vampire story surfaced. Was there a chance those vampires were for real? Had she driven them away from their homes? No, she wouldn't think about that now. She had to stay focused on Taurin and what he was offering.

"I'll be recording our sessions. How do you feel about that?" This was the last hurdle. "Oh, and don't worry about the park's reputation, because I'll make sure the public knows this stuff wasn't sanctioned by the management. It's just that the park does such a great job with its fantasies that people get carried away." That should ease any guilt he was feeling about ratting out his employers.

"No problem as long as you don't use my name." His expression gave nothing away.

Now that the business side of the discussion was over, she didn't know what to say. She had a thousand questions about his life as a vampire, but she'd wait until they were on their way back to the castle. Something about the moon-lit beach didn't lend itself to work-related chatter.

"So, I guess we can go back to the castle now." The adrenaline rush had worn off, and reality smacked her right in the face. Dark, empty beach. Dark, dangerous vampire sitting beside her. *Feet, take me outta here.* Only her feet couldn't take her anywhere until her behind decided it wanted to move away from his sexy presence. Her bottom was perfectly happy.

He watched her from eyes that shone in the night. "Don't be in such a hurry, Kristin. Enjoy the moment."

She made a big show of drawing in a deep breath of sea air, scooping up a handful of sand, and staring for a moment at the dark waves breaking on the shore. "Okay, enjoyed the moment. We can go now." When had she morphed into a giant wuss?

"In a big hurry to get away, aren't you, sweetheart? We haven't sealed the deal yet." His smile was slow, hot, and *knowing*.

"Sealed the deal?" Her voice reached for a higher octave. She was trying for I'm-cool-with-creatures, but her voice wasn't a good liar.

His sensual smile slid into a frown. "You sound nervous. Guess I can understand that. I won't lie to you, all the nonhumans in the castle have a potential for violence, but only when provoked." His smile returned. "Thinking of provoking me, lady?"

Oooh, yes. "I don't provoke vampires. So how are we going to seal the deal?" Did she really need to know this? Uh-uh. Did she *want* to know it? Definitely.

He leaned toward her, blocking out the pale moonlight with his broad shoulders. Broad *bare* shoulders. She couldn't help it; she ran her fingers across his chest, savoring the tactile sensation of smooth warm skin over hard muscle.

And when he lowered his head to cover her mouth with his, she opened her lips to him without even once thinking about how she'd describe this scene in her article.

His lips were warm on hers, and he tasted of gulf breezes and potent sensuality just too yummy to resist. But then, who was resisting?

He nipped her lower lip before moving away from her. Rats. Kristin had just begun to involve all her senses. She'd explored the texture of him—the smoothness of his mouth, the softness of his lips, and when she'd wrapped her arms around him, the strong contours of his back. He hadn't given her nearly enough time. The senses that had missed their turns were in the middle of a major bitch-fest.

Kristin took the hand he offered and let him pull her to her feet. "Not much of a deal-sealing. We didn't even get to the part where we cut our wrists and do the blood-brother thing." She thought about that. "Yeah, maybe that wouldn't be a good idea. Wouldn't want you to get overexcited or anything."

Something primitive and hot moved in his eyes as he walked beside her to his car. "Trust me, I was excited." He looked away from her. "A lot."

Well, that sounded promising. She was ridiculously pleased with herself. Which was really stupid, because an excited vampire would probably have the hots for her neck. Not a good thing for her neck—or connected body parts.

Once in the car, she drowned out her mind's early-warning system with her favorite thing—words. "So how old are you, and who made you vampire?"

Silence.

"How often do you have to feed, and do you prefer blood banks or the occasional tourist?"

Silence.

"How do you feel about the extended-life thing, and does it bother you to never see daylight?"

Silence.

Kristin leaned her head back against the seat's headrest and sighed loudly. "Well, that was a productive little chat."

He drove in silence for a few more minutes before speaking. "Why should I tell you about myself? You might decide to use it."

She tried to sound outraged even as her conscience made a cameo appearance. "We have a deal. You can trust me." Her conscience looked suspiciously like her long-departed Grandma Hughes. Grandma shook her head sadly. Kristin felt guilty. Grandma did guilt well.

Taurin seemed to consider her answer. "I was born in Italy six hundred years ago. My brother, Dacian, made me vampire."

Kristin felt righteous indignation on Taurin's behalf. "Bummer. Not much of a brother."

"He was the best brother a man could have." When Taurin glanced at her, his belief in his brother gleamed fierce in his eyes. "I was dying, and he made me vampire so I'd survive."

Whoa, touchy subject. "Where's Dacian now?"

"I don't know. For centuries I thought he'd died in a fire that Eric had set. I stalked Eric, planning how I'd kill him. Turns out, Dacian used the fire to stage his own disappearance. If everyone thought he was dead, no one would search for him." He shrugged. "I just got back from trying to find him. No luck."

Kristin had never thought of herself as particularly sensitive to the emotions of others, but she recognized the hurt that lay beneath his casual shrug, a deep well of regret that the brother he loved had chosen to walk away from him. She felt Taurin's pain as a surprising stab of sorrow in her own heart. *Not* what she wanted to feel. Lust was okay, because he was a spectacular male animal. But sorrow for his pain was a little deeper, a little more worrisome.

"Umm, I have ways of finding people. Maybe I could help." Did she just say that? No, she wouldn't be that stupid. But it had sort of sounded like her. Well, hell.

Hope flared in his eyes and then was gone. "Thanks, but if Dacian doesn't want to be found, he won't be." He parked the car, and they got out. "I'll see you to your room."

Kristin was the one who remained silent all the way to her door. He didn't realize it, but he'd thrown down a gauntlet. Once she was alone, she'd get on her laptop and see what she could find out about Dacian. . . . "What's your last name? You never mentioned it." She unlocked her door, pushed it open, and then stood in the doorway waiting for his answer.

He stared at her for a little too long. A squiggle of unease worked its way up her spine.

She recognized the exact moment he decided to tell her. His smile was all wicked anticipation.

"My last name is Veris." Turning away, he disappeared down the dark stairway.

Calmly, she stepped into her room, closed the door, and then leaned her forehead against it.

"Wonderful."

CHAPTER ◆ FIVE

Taurin slammed out of his room and headed for the stairs to the great hall. He'd messed up big-time. What the hell had he been thinking last night? Just for the momentary joy of watching the expression on Kristin's face, he'd played his trump card. He'd told her his last name.

How dumb was that? Taurin didn't think she'd leave. She wanted her freakin' story too much. But she wouldn't want to get it from him. He could see her taking practice swings with a lamp just in case he was crazy enough to show up at her door. Yeah, she'd be pissed. He'd made her life miserable after she wrote that vampire story. But she'd deserved it.

Somehow the she-deserved-it line didn't make him feel any better. Taurin reached the great hall and looked around. He didn't see any of his friends, but he saw something else that made him growl low in his throat—Kristin dressed in shorts and a sexy little top. And she was standing by the door talking to Banan.

If anyone had asked him right then what color those shorts and sexy top were, he'd have said red. Taurin was seeing lots of red as he strode toward the two.

He came to a stop facing Kristin and smiled at her. It probably wasn't a great grin because he was preparing to duck. "Ready for tonight's fantasy?"

The smile she turned on him was a mere lifting of her lips with no emotion attached. "Sure. Banan showed me around the park today, so I'm ready for the night." Her gaze gave nothing away.

His sure did. He glared at the shark.

The shark smiled with all his teeth on display. "Yeah, Kristin and I had a great time. She said tomorrow night we could go for a swim because she wants to see me change."

Over my undead body. "Wouldn't pencil that into your schedule just yet. The park has lots of attractions, and Kristin and I have to experience them all before she leaves." Taurin fixed his unblinking stare on Banan. "She'll probably be too busy to do much swimming."

Banan looked amused. "We'll see." He turned his attention back to Kristin. "Today was fun. Looking forward to tomorrow." Ignoring Taurin's glower, he walked away.

"Fascinating man." Kristin sounded thoughtful. "And a lonely man, I'd guess. He doesn't have any close friends. Not many people want to get close to someone whose alternate form is a great white."

"He's a predator." Taurin didn't want her thinking about

Banan, feeling sorry for Banan, feeling *anything* for Banan. The fierceness of his jealousy blew him away.

"So are you." Nothing in her inflection hinted at her emotions.

Taurin figured she had to be ticked at him. So where was the temper? "Yeah, but I don't sneak up on people and rip off limbs."

"You just drain them dry." Some bitterness finally seeped through. "Or rip out their hearts. Metaphorically speaking, of course."

"Rip out their hearts? Getting a little melodramatic, aren't we, sweetheart? Look, we have to go somewhere and talk about this." So he'd messed with her career a little. He had to make her understand the damage she'd caused with her story.

She nodded and then followed him out of the castle. They walked in silence until they reached the Sea World Fantasy.

"We can start here." He'd already made arrangements to use one of the mock mini-submarines for as long as they needed it. "This'll give us privacy."

Kristin didn't say anything as she climbed into the small sub. Taurin climbed in after her, closed the hatch, hit a switch, and started the virtual descent into the equally virtual sea.

She didn't notice when he opened a small panel by the hatch and turned a key. There, no interruptions until they were ready to leave. The sub rocked gently as water seemed to rise past the windows.

"Cool." She wandered around the small area, inspecting the instrument panel and the two cockpit-type seats in front of it. Beyond the panel was a large wraparound window that gave a panoramic view of the sea and sea bottom. "Very realistic."

Okay, time to start giving her the info she wanted. "Once a couple gets down here, they don't pay much attention to what's going on outside." He took a deep breath. She wanted kinky, so he'd take it over the top. "I remember a woman who came in with three guys. They all squeezed into this one sub. Then—"

"You know you're a slime-sucking toad, don't you?" Kristin turned to face him. She used the same tone she'd use to tell him they were having asparagus for dinner.

Looked like the kinky sex story would have to wait. "Yeah, but you did a job on a lot of lives."

"Give me a break. I didn't *know* you guys were the real deal." She flung her arms into the air as her voice rose. Her calm façade was cracking. "You almost ruined my whole career."

Fine, she wanted mad, he'd give her mad. "Some of those vampires had lived in San Antonio for more than a hundred years, pretending they were their own children when people started to ask questions. Do you know how hard it was to pick up and leave a city they loved?" He was doing some shouting of his own now. "But what would you care? All you want is the story, no matter who it hurts."

"That's not true." Her cheeks were flushed.

She was cute when she was steamed. Probably wouldn't

want to hear that right now. Fish swam past the windows, but she was too focused on her mad to notice.

"Could've fooled me." Jeez, he was getting soft. He shouldn't be thinking about cute and Kristin in the same sentence. "I bet even as we speak you're scheming to double-cross me. You're greedy. You want both stories to hawk to every sleazy publisher in the country."

"I'm not." Her denial sounded a little weak to him.

Dammit, he'd bet that's exactly what she had planned. Without thinking, he slipped into her thoughts to verify his suspicion. Aha, he was right.

Uh-oh. He shouldn't have done that. As he withdrew from her mind, he watched her warily. Eric could tiptoe into a person's thoughts and go undetected. Not him. When he was in a mind he may as well be wearing hobnailed boots.

She narrowed her eyes, her anger beating against him. "I felt that. You were in my mind. You told me you couldn't read people's thoughts. So beside everything else, you're a worm-eating liar."

Yeah, she'd noticed. "Good thing I checked. Guess I'll have to tell Eric to dust off that pink eraser."

Kristin couldn't remember ever being this angry. She was furious about what he'd tried to do to her career. She was ticked about him invading her thoughts. But most of all, she was upset that he'd exposed her plan to use both stories. Not because she wouldn't get them, but because his accusation made her feel like the lowlife he thought she was.

When in doubt, attack. She moved in on him, nose to chest. Not too intimidating, but she'd have to stand on something to do the nose-to-nose thing. Kristin settled for jabbing him in the chest with her finger.

"Let me tell you something, bloodsucker. I—" She caught a glimpse of something moving just outside the window.

Turning her head, she stared into eyes as big as dinner plates. Holy cow! Monstrous tentacles waved at her. Even as she widened her eyes to take in the full horror of the thing, the super-sized octopus attached said tentacles to the window with a menacing *thwup*, *thwup* of its many suction cups.

And in the time-honored tradition of all kick-butt heroines, she screamed like a demented fire siren. "Aaiigh!" Then she flung herself at Taurin. Wrapping her arms and legs around him, she hung on. Hey, kick-butt heroines know about that living-to-fight-another-day stuff.

Taurin evidently wasn't prepared for her . . . enthusiastic response, because he went down with her riding him all the way.

While her heart clawed its way up her throat, she tried to jump-start her brain cells. *Notreal, notreal.* Meanwhile, there was upheaval below. She looked down. Taurin was laughing at her.

"I *never* lose it that way." She should move, but she was still shaking.

"Right. The same way you never faint." Taurin's laughter faded, and his gaze heated.

Emotion flooded her as she raised a shaking hand to rake her hair away from her face. "It's every damn thing that's happened to me here. All of it just balled up inside of me— vampires, shape-shifters, and God knows what else—so when I saw the octopus I just came apart."

The reality of the last three days washed over her. Horrified, she felt tears sliding down her face. She opened her mouth to tell him she never cried, but then shut it. Like he'd believe her.

"Hey, it's okay." He clasped her shoulders and pulled her down until she lay flat on top of him. "No one blames you for feeling jumpy. You should've seen me when I first realized vampires existed. I hid in a cave for a week."

Kristin looked down at his face, so close to hers, and she knew her eyes were still awash in tears. "Really?"

"Well, maybe not a whole week. Dacian dragged me out after three days." As he spoke, he rubbed his hands up and down her back in a comforting rhythm.

Well, *he* might think it was comforting, but she was feeling something else entirely. Strong emotions fed other strong emotions. Now that she'd released some of her stress in that stupid outburst, she could appreciate her position.

Pressed flat against his muscular length, she felt every tiny movement of his body. As he shifted his position to pull her closer, her nipples scraped across his chest, immediately raising false hopes in areas farther south.

While her brain tried to convince everyone to calm down, that this was just a random meeting of nipples and yummy male chest, the rest of her body knew better.

So did *his* body. She felt his growing interest in the most basic way. Mmm. The instinctive upward thrust of his hips triggered pressure low in her belly.

Tentatively, she slid back and forth over *his* ridge of high pressure—who knew weather forecasts could be sexy?—forcing a gasp from him. There was so much pressure building that she just knew a storm couldn't be far behind.

With a muttered curse, he put his hands on either side of her face and pulled her close to meet his kiss. She'd been right. The sexual wind he generated picked her up, sucked her into its vortex, and carried her away from life's little concerns. Like if you kiss a vampire, will he respect you in the morning? More to the point, will you even be alive in the morning?

Too late for any deep thoughts about survival. She was into the moment. Her tongue tangled with his, and his taste was so hungry male that she clenched around the delicious pleasure it brought her. Oh, yesss. Without any preplanning, she checked for fangs with the tip of her tongue and found them. She smoothed her tongue over the length of each one. There was something wickedly sensual about the action.

Hey, if she got such a rush from sliding her tongue over just his fangs, who knew what erotic thrills awaited if she put her mouth on other parts of his body?

He kissed a path down the side of her jaw and neck. When she felt his breath warm on her throat, a teeny, tiny twinge of self-preservation kicked in.

She raised her head and smiled down at him. "Your eyes haven't changed, just your teeth."

He smiled back at her. "I'm hanging on to my control, sweetheart, but it's tough."

Was she weird for finding the implied threat of those fangs sort of a turn-on? Maybe she wouldn't write about this scene in her article. "So sexual excitement triggers the change?"

May as well keep busy while she asked questions. Kristin sat up and then grabbed the bottom of his T-shirt. He obliged by lifting his torso so she could pull the shirt over his head.

Then she scooted down his prone body so that when she leaned over, she had full access to that incredible chest. She sampled one nipple with the tip of her tongue. His groan was all she could hope for.

"Making love in vampire form takes the whole experience to another level." He seemed to be having trouble wrapping his tongue around his words. No wonder, considering how hard his tongue had just worked.

"In other words, you have to bite someone to achieve complete sexual satisfaction." Why was she talking? She had better things to do with her mouth—she ran her fingers lightly over his broad chest—and her hands.

"Uh-huh. But don't worry. I've had centuries to learn control. You're safe." He reached up to slide the straps of her top off her shoulders.

Too bad. Kristin blinked. That thought had surprised even her. No, definitely didn't want him attaching himself to her neck with those shiny fangs. Teeth in neck would be a major owie.

Taurin pulled her top down to her waist and with what had to be an amazing feat of preternatural speed, whipped off her bra. It was her turn to groan as he rolled her nipples between his fingers.

Focus. They were losing control. *Heeere, control, control.* She was *letting* them get out of control. In fact, she was a major contributor to their out-of-control state.

Before she could decide a wise course of action, he pulled her down until he could reach her breasts with his mouth. He circled each nipple with the tip of his finger, and then drew the first one into the heat of his mouth. And by the time he'd worked his magic on both with his teeth and tongue, she was whimpering.

To hell with being wise. She was planted on top of his erection. What was the old truism—use it or lose it? Made a whole lot of sense to her.

Reaching down, she fumbled with the buttons on his jeans. "It's summer. Aren't you hot in jeans?"

"I'm hotter without them." To demonstrate, he reached down to help her with the buttons, and then slid them off along with his shorts.

Ohmigod! So long, so thick, so hard, so *wonderful*. Every sexual cell in her body contracted into a tight ball of want. He was temptation on a scale not seen since Eve ate that blasted apple. In fact, if Taurin had done the tempting, Eve would've shaken every apple from that tree and taken them all home to make applesauce.

Kristin had knelt up to give him room to shuck his jeans, but now she couldn't help herself, she lowered herself onto his erection and ground herself into him. He pressed between her spread legs and only her shorts and panties kept her from impaling herself on him.

His control must've been slipping fast because his eyes grew larger and darker with that telltale slant. But there wasn't any room in her sex-clogged brain for fear.

He half-sat and then reached behind her to slip his hands under her shorts and panties. He cupped her cheeks and kneaded with deep, firm strokes.

The waist of her shorts wasn't up to the strain of a pair of male hands stretching it to its limit. The button holding the shorts closed popped off and rolled across the floor. Who needed buttons anyway?

A diver had replaced the octopus at the sub's window. Who cared? A whole team of Navy SEALs could be staring in for all she cared.

Suddenly Taurin abandoned his kneading and collapsed back onto the floor. He rested the back of his hand across his eyes. "Damn, damn, damn."

"What?" Why was he lying down on the job? Her heart was racing, and she was wet with the anticipation of him sliding deep inside her.

"No protection." His disappointment was a harsh groan.

She stared down at him, outrage out of all proportion to his crime narrowing her eyes. "How could you forget? You can read minds. You can move at the speed of the mail bringing my credit card bills to me, for heaven sake."

Wait. She blinked. Wasn't she supposed to be mad at him? She could've sworn that he was a yucky slug. Kristin just couldn't remember why.

Glancing away from Taurin, she tried to rein in her runaway emotions and sexual want. Her gaze slid to the sub's large window. The diver had left. She stared. Something else had taken his place. It was big, and white, and had lots and lots of sharp teeth. And the laughter gleaming in its dark fishy eyes was all too human.

"Umm. I think Banan is trying to get our attention." Keeping her gaze fixed on the shark, she reached for her top and slipped into it. She stuffed her bra down the back of her shorts.

"Banan?" Taurin sat up partway and supported himself on

his elbows as he twisted to stare at the window. He snarled at the shark. "That's not water outside the window, so he's standing there in human form while he projects his shark image to us. I'll kill him."

"He can do that?" Once again the awesome powers of the beings she'd met so far boggled her mind.

"Evidently." Taurin sat the rest of the way up. "We're not seeing the shark with our eyes. We're seeing it up here." He tapped his forehead.

Kristin glanced back at the window. Sure enough, Banan in human form was standing there waving at them. Suddenly, she realized where her bottom was planted and slid off Taurin. He reached for his jeans.

Without even a warning knock, someone lifted the hatch, and Saffron leaped through the opening. He took in everything at a glance and then padded over to Taurin. "Tell me you weren't on the bottom. Real men do it on top."

Fury rolled off Taurin in waves. Kristin didn't need any superpowers to feel it. She clambered to her feet and edged away from Saffron. One didn't stand near a tree about to be chopped down, because you never knew where it would fall.

"Real cats know when they're about to lose one of their nine lives and run like hell." Taurin lifted his lips away from fangs that looked a lot scarier now that Kristin wasn't in a sexual frenzy.

Saffron seemed to realize that maybe his entrance had been a little precipitous. Every hair on his fluffy white body stood on end, and his tail puffed up to twice its normal size. He looked like a furry snowball.

"Hey, man, I was just riding to your rescue. You were in

here a long time, and the hatch was locked from inside. Everyone was worried that maybe something had happened to you guys."

"And *everyone* was?" Kristin was with Taurin on this. If she had fangs, she'd be flashing them.

"Uh, I guess Banan and me. Real men act when they think someone's in danger, so we decided to make sure you didn't need saving." Saffron backed toward the open hatch. "Banan said he'd look in the window, and I opened the hatch. Locks don't stop me."

Taurin was in full furious-vampire form. He hissed at Saffron. "You both wanted to see what you could see. Okay, satisfied? Question, cat, who's going to save *you*?"

"I'll take him off your hands." Asima poked her aristocratic head through the hatch. *"Oh, I left your scarf in your room, Kristin."* There was a brilliant white flash of light, and both cats were gone.

A quick glance assured Kristin that Banan was also gone. She thought about turning her back while Taurin dressed, but decided she'd be better served by getting her last big hit of his magnificent bare body.

Because now that her heartbeat had slowed and her breathing was kind of normal, she realized what she'd almost done. The scary part? She regretted the "almost" part. Her mind knew that any involvement with Taurin Veris was bad news, but her body wanted what it wanted, and that was that. She was in trouble.

"I guess a better man would say he was sorry that happened." His smile was slow, wicked, and totally sensual. "Guess that's not me."

Guess that wasn't *her*, either. She was doing a great job of compartmentalizing. What he'd done to her career still outraged her—even though she understood the why of it—but that didn't keep her from wanting to be with him, and she definitely still wanted his body. At what point would the wall between the two compartments spring a leak, and would the resulting mix freeze into a block of ice or go up in flames?

Kristin sighed. She was betting on the flames. "So what will I take away from this for my article?" She climbed from the sub and then waited for Taurin to join her. "You never finished the story about the woman and the three guys."

He walked beside her back toward the castle. No way was she going on to another attraction with her bra stuck down the back of her shorts.

"After their time in the sub was up, only the woman came out." Taurin glanced at her and smiled. "The park employee in charge of the attraction went into the sub to see what had happened."

"And?" Kristin hoped the punch line to this story was great, because she needed something fantastic to make up for her sexual frustration tonight.

"The three men were chained to the instrument panel."

"Whoa." This was good stuff.

"Naked."

"Wow, bet they were embarrassed." Kristin couldn't wait to get back to her room so she could write this up.

"Don't think so. They were all smiling."

And as Taurin held the door of the castle open for her, she tried not to think of his bare muscular body chained to her very own instrument panel.

CHAPTER ◆ SIX

"So, how are things going?" Sparkle perched on the stool behind her candy counter. She crossed her legs as she stared at Deimos, who was nervously rubbing the top of his shiny shaved head.

Her nails were perfect, her shoes were perfect, her dress was perfect, and she was perfectly bored. She missed the challenge, the excitement of meddling in the sexual lives of the people around her. But Deimos had to do this himself, hence, no meddling.

Maybe he'd fail miserably, and then she'd step in to save the day. The thought cheered her right up.

Deimos abandoned his head to lean casually against the candy counter. He was trying hard to look calm and in control, but Sparkle recognized the trapped-rabbit look in the way his gaze skittered around the store.

Sparkle smiled. Good. If Kristin and Taurin had already

had sex, Deimos wouldn't be nervous. As soon as he got up the courage to tell her he'd screwed everything up, she'd graciously offer to take over the operation. He'd be childishly grateful to her. Life would be good again.

Deimos finally met her gaze, and she didn't like what she saw there. He looked almost defiant. She scowled.

"Everything's under control. I'm working it. See, I remembered what you said about sexual tension."

Amazing. Something she'd said had actually sunk in. "Uh-huh. And you're using that info how?"

"The beach party's tonight. Kristin and Taurin have done a fantasy every night this past week. But each time they've gotten close to making love, Saffron or Banan has interrupted them. Once they tried to hole up in her room, but Banan pulled the fire alarm. Nothing like a fire alarm to get a vamp out of the mood." He grinned at the memory. "They're so hot for each other I can smell the fire." Deimos waved his arms to give her a leaping flames visual.

"And?" Sparkle was intrigued in spite of herself.

"Well, tonight will be the night they finally do it. I mean, this will be one sexy beach party. They have so much pent-up sexual energy that it'll just explode."

"Interesting." Sparkle thought about how she could impact the party's sexual energy in her own small way. "Oh, and get over the 'making love' thing. They're having sex. Love doesn't have anything to do with it."

Deimos looked thoughtful for a moment. "No, I think you're wrong. They really like each other. Oh, Kristin still thinks she's mad at him because of what he did to her career, and he still thinks she's all about the story, but I almost think they're in love. Go figure."

"Hmm." Surprise, surprise. It took a lot of guts to tell Sparkle Stardust she was wrong. He might make a worthy cosmic troublemaker after all. "How have Kristin and Taurin reacted to all those interruptions?"

Deimos frowned for the first time. "Taurin said he'd tear out someone's throat if either Saffron or Banan showed up again. Kristin said she suspected a mastermind behind this whole thing, because it seemed orchestrated to her. She threatened to use her investigative skills to ferret out the one in control."

"Not good." Sparkle tapped one perfect nail on the glass top of her counter. "But they'll be too busy thinking about each other tonight to worry about anything else. Just out of curiosity, how'd you convince Saffron and Banan to play your game?"

Deimos fixed his gaze on a spot somewhere above her head. "I promised them a date with you."

"Excellent. I like it when you show initiative because . . ." She stopped tapping her nail. "You *what*?"

He rushed into his explanation. Deimos knew when death was a hair's breadth away. "They both think you're hot, and really really admire your . . . mind. All they want is one date so they can explore . . ." Deimos's creative lying powers finally deserted him.

"I *know* what they want to explore." She studied him with narrow-eyed intensity.

Sparkle didn't like the idea of being the prize in this particular game, but she had to admit that Deimos had shown a certain amount of flair and ingenuity. And courage. Lots of courage. Because he knew exactly what could happen if he pissed her off.

"A date, huh? Banan is a sexy guy, so I won't mind exploring possibilities with him. Saffron's a cat of a different color though. I don't have a clue what he looks like in human form. I do know he's got this thing about men being the dominant sex." She knew her smile was a wicked twist of her lips. "Maybe a date with Saffron would be fun. I can teach him sooo much about women."

Deimos's expression said he wouldn't trade places with Saffron even for the chance to be an action hero.

"Go do your thing." Sparkle waved him toward the door.

Once he'd left, she studied her nails for a long time. She always did her best thinking while contemplating her nails or a new pair of shoes.

Finally she looked up and smiled. Deimos would have the glory tonight, but she couldn't resist adding a little twist to the end of the story.

Sparkle picked up her cell phone and punched in a number. Tonight would be spectacular. "Let the games begin."

Kristin stood on the beach wondering when exactly during the past week she'd been flung into an alternate universe. She glanced up at the night sky. Yep, that full moon looked like her world's moon. She lowered her gaze to the silver-tipped waves rolling onto the beach. Sure looked like the Gulf of Mexico to her.

Then she turned her attention to the man walking toward her across the sand. Nope, he definitely wasn't part of her world's reality, because in the reality she knew, she'd never fall in love with a vampire.

Why had it happened? Sure he was gorgeous, but it had to be something more to shift the whole thing from lust to love. They'd talked a lot. They'd argued and laughed together. And when she'd told him she'd found a clue to his brother's whereabouts, she'd gotten all teary-eyed at his excitement.

How did she know her love was for real? She'd deleted both of her stories from her laptop tonight. Didn't get more in love than that. Of course, what she felt didn't mean squat, because Taurin hadn't hinted he felt the same. Yeah, he wanted her body, but he didn't want her heart and soul as part of a package deal. She sat down on the blanket he'd spread on the sand and waited for him.

He stopped in front of her and handed her a glass of iced tea along with a plate that had a burger, potato salad, and a chocolate chip cookie on it. Then he dropped down beside her.

Kristin could see the glow from the fire someone had built on the beach, but a dune hid Taurin and her from view.

"Looks like Banan and Saffron are stuffing their faces. Should keep them busy for a while." He didn't need to add that they should take advantage of their window of opportunity.

Kristin wanted to think of herself as a romantic, but she had a big, bold, practical streak running right down the middle of all that pink lacy romanticism.

"Protection?" If the heat he generated wasn't burning up all her brain cells, she would've remembered to bring some herself.

She had a sinking feeling that his little foil packets were sitting back on his night table, because unless he had them tucked in his cheeks like a sexy chipmunk, he was out of pocket options. She knew, because she'd looked.

And there was so much to look at. His swimsuit was an insignificant punctuation mark to the complex sentence that was his body. Smooth, muscular, and almost bare, his was a body to launch the sexual dreams of a thousand women.

The moonlight played with the angles and curves of him, casting some in shadow—teasing and tempting— while highlighting others just enough to make her want to reach out so she could make sure he was real.

She had to have him, and she had to have him *now*. "Umm, do you think Eric or Conall might have—"

Leaning over, he placed his finger over her lips. He should know better than to put any part of his body near her mouth when she was in a serious state of wanting. Grasping his wrist so he couldn't escape, she drew his finger into her mouth. Swirling her tongue around it, she met his sizzling gaze. He tasted of chocolate chip cookie, her new favorite dessert.

"Keep that up, sweetheart, and I'll forget something

very important I have to tell you." He gripped his bottom lip between his strong white teeth.

And when he released his lip, its sheen and soft fullness called to the savage Amazon in her. She wanted to visit unspeakably erotic acts on his helpless body. Not that she figured his body would be helpless any time soon.

She couldn't talk while she lavished all her uncontrolled desire on his finger, so she released him. "This better be good, Veris."

He grinned as he stretched out flat on his back beside her. Then he slid his palm over his chest and abdomen, calling attention to his powerful pecs and abs.

She'd bitten into her cookie in lieu of anything else yummy to sink her teeth into as she watched him slide his fingers over his body. Completely riveted, she carelessly dribbled a few cookie crumbs onto him.

He paused in his epic journey. "Uh-uh. Littering isn't allowed. You've seen the signs: Don't Mess with Texas."

Kristin looked down at the scattering of crumbs. "Oops. Gotta do my part in keeping Texas tidy."

She shivered at the joy of being a one-woman cleanup crew. Bending close to him, she flicked a crumb from his nipple with the tip of her tongue. To make absolutely sure she'd gotten the entire crumb, she gripped his nipple gently with her teeth and then brushed her tongue back and forth, back and forth over the sensitive nub. He groaned his appreciation.

With what she hoped was a maddeningly slow pace, she put her mouth on random parts of his torso. Some stops had crumbs that she flicked up with her tongue, some didn't. No matter, because she was into the feel of his warm flesh beneath her lips, the taste of essential male on her tongue, and the scent of an aroused, sexy man.

When she finally abandoned his body, he glanced down to where his hand still rested on his lower abdomen. "I know I was going somewhere, but now it's all a blur."

Kristin made a wild impetuous guess at his final destination and decided to help. "Let me drive for a while."

He shifted his hips as he settled in for the trip. She sucked in her breath at the sensual impact of watching the thin swimsuit material stretch tightly over his growing interest.

Kristin walked her fingers around the edge of his swimsuit, making sure she didn't ignore where it marked the border between his inner thighs and protected territory. He spread his legs to make the journey easier.

"Taking the scenic route is always more rewarding, don't you think?" She walked her fingers across his personal Mount Everest that was gaining elevation even as she spoke.

She interpreted his grunt as a negative. "You're right. Time to head home." Slipping her fingers beneath the edge of his swimsuit, she paused. Then laughed as she pulled out two foil packets. "Now that we have these, you really don't need the swimsuit, do you?" Kristin tugged at the waist.

His smile was a predatory lifting of his lips. "I thought you'd never ask." He arched his hips so she could skim the swimsuit from his body. Then he reached up to hook his finger in her bikini top. "Take it off."

"Wow. Pretty direct, aren't you?" Kristin kind of liked that about him. She looked down. Mmm. The hard length of him went *way* beyond like.

He sat up, his eyes a blaze of hunger that made her nipples pebble without him even touching her. "I've spent a week in hell, wanting to rip the clothes from your beautiful body and bury myself deep inside you every freakin' minute I've been near you."

Kristin knew her smile bordered on feral. "Whoa. Intense. Very sexy." She dropped her hand to his erection and wrapped her fingers around him. She squeezed gently, instant messaging a "Me, too."

He pulled her close so he could untie her top. She was short on control right now. His fault, all his fault. Jeez, how long did it take to untie a stupid bikini top? To keep from attacking him, she clamped her teeth onto his neck and hung on. She reveled in the warmth and taste of his skin. Would he accept her teeth's imprints in the spirit they were given? She hoped so. Who knew this vampire stuff would be so easy?

Even before her top hit the sand, he was working on her bikini bottom. He must've used his preternatural speed or something because one minute it was there and then it was lying yards away. Was he hot for her or what? She smiled at the delicious thought.

Kristin glanced around to make sure they were completely private before relaxing back onto the blanket. Lifting her arms above her head, she stretched, arching her back and savoring the sensual joy of the cool gulf breeze and Taurin's heated gaze drifting across her bare breasts. She glanced at his strong hands with fingers able to drift over a woman's body in many different ways. Who needed a breeze?

Leaning close, he traced her lips with his tongue and then deepened the kiss into a promise of things to come. Kristin thought whatever was to come better come damn fast, because no way did she intend to give Banan or Saffron time to interrupt this.

Taurin grinned at her, his fangs proof of his own state of arousal. "Don't worry, if they interrupt tonight I'll kill them. No one will find the bodies. What happens in Galveston stays in Galveston."

She thought he was only half kidding. "Were you in my head? I didn't feel you."

Still holding her gaze, he moved to kneel between her legs. "Nope. I recognized that mess-with-my-orgasm-and-die look in your eyes." He slid his hands over her feet, gently massaging her heels before smoothing his palms over her calves and inner thighs. He paused there. "I want to make long, slow love to you. I want to show you every single thing I've learned in six hundred years about bringing a woman pleasure."

He leaned over to whisper in her ear. "But not tonight. I want you too much. I want to take you fast and hard with lots of thrashing around and screams for more."

She tangled her fingers in his hair and pulled him down to her. "Do it. But we'd better delete the screams. Unless we want an audience who'll break into spontaneous applause with shouts for an encore." Kristin trailed her fingers down the long length of his back before massaging the cheeks of his perfect ass.

"Hey, that's not a bad fantasy. Maybe we should—"

Kristin slapped that perfect ass. "No audience."

"I love it when you act tough, woman." His sexy murmur was pure seduction by sound waves.

He splayed his fingers over her stomach, and she felt her stomach muscles quiver in response to his touch. Jeez, if her stomach muscles got this excited, what would happen when he touched parts of her body given to nervous fits? She found out fast.

Taurin put both hands over her breasts, and she let the sensation of weight and heat seep through her. Then he did what she'd expected. He put his mouth on her breast. Not that she'd mark him down for lack of creativity. After all, there were just so many things a guy could do to a woman that would . . .

Oh. My. God! He nipped, he flicked with his tongue—who knew the tongue could do so many things—and he used just enough suction to drive her berserk. "That's . . . That's . . ." Her body was on the launchpad, and the countdown had begun.

And somewhere, what remained of her analytical mind understood that because she loved him, her body automatically super-sized the pleasure every time he touched her.

At some point she realized he was no longer touching her breasts. Her nipples were still warm and wet from his mouth, and the breeze felt almost chilly moving over them. But the breeze sure wasn't cooling down her other parts.

He sounded unsure as he looked down at her. "Will you trust me to enter your mind, Kristin?" Something in his gaze said her trust was important to him.

Did she trust him? Love and trust went together as far as she was concerned. If she invited him into her body, couldn't she also invite him into her mind this once? "Yes."

She played her fingers over his sweat-sheened stomach and watched his muscles contract. *She* was doing this to him, and she hadn't even gotten started yet. Kristin figured she'd need at least a few centuries to exhaust all the ways she wanted to touch him.

"I want to join my mind with yours as we make love." He didn't smile, his gaze searing her with his need. "I won't tell you what to expect because that would spoil the fun." Then he did smile, slow and provocative. If a smile could trigger an orgasm, his would.

Kristin would've worried about what was going to happen, but he didn't give her a chance. He licked his way down her body, and as heat pooled low in her belly, she felt a surge of emotion—overwhelming pleasure and intense arousal. Not hers. *Theirs.* She growled low in her throat. She didn't growl. Ever.

She spread her thighs wide to accept him. And just in case he missed his stop, Kristin had a virtual "You have reached your destination" sign planted in the driveway. Bending her knees, she lifted her hips to meet his imagined thrust. Then she reached down and touched herself, sensually and with lots of special effects. "I'm waiting for you, vampire." Was that low sexy voice hers? Wow.

Taurin raised his head to stare at her. *"I love you, Kristin. I'm telling you now so you can't accuse me of saying it in a postorgasmic haze. I've never shared a woman's mind while making love, never wanted to. You're the first, the last."*

Kristin's breath caught in her throat. He'd just said he loved her in her mind. She opened her mouth to tell him she loved him, too, but he shook his head. "Shh."

"Later, Kristin. When you have time to think, to understand that you'll grow old and I won't, that you'll still walk in daylight, but I won't." His smile hung somewhere between hopeful and sad. *"But there would be lots of perks, like this."*

He knelt up, clasped her bottom, and lifted her to meet his mouth. She wrapped her legs around him as he slid the tip of his tongue back and forth across *that* spot. She swallowed her screams and almost choked on them. Added to her own unbearable sensations was his spiraling pleasure filling and overflowing her mind.

And when he slid his tongue into her and then out, in and out, in and out, she couldn't keep a whimper from escaping. Her body shuddered under the force of their combined physical and emotional arousals.

Enough! "Nownownow." She grabbed his hair, forcing him to slide up her body. The friction was so hot she expected to see smoke rising from between them.

He took ten years, er, seconds to do the protection thing. Way too long.

She was mindless, nothing more than a pounding heart, ragged breathing, and senses that were stripped to bare-wire essentials. As he rose over her, she wrapped her legs around his waist, and waited for the nudge of his shaft.

Taurin spread her, easing into her, pushing deeper and deeper, claiming her. His emotions were silent moans in her head. Deeper, and still deeper. Her body clenched around all that hard length, and she joined his mental shouts of pleasure with her own.

Then he started to move. He slid out until only the head of his shaft remained inside her before plunging into her over and over again. She experienced right along with him the almost unbearable friction driving him to thrust faster and faster, felt her own orgasm gathering power, and teetered on the edge.

But when she felt the slide of his fangs against her throat she stilled. He waited silently for her decision. Riding her sensual high, Kristin didn't have to do any deep thinking. She trusted him. "Do it, vampire."

If there was pain, she didn't feel it, because the instant surge in erotic sensation was a sexual body slam.

"We have liftoff." Kristin didn't know if she'd said it out loud, didn't care, because her orgasm grabbed her and shook her until she dug her fingers into his back and hung on. Taurin's release went on, and on, and on in her head. She only hoped her shouts were also in her head.

Her last thought before mindless ecstasy took over was that she didn't know if she could live through this two-orgasms-at-once thing.

She lived. Barely. Her breathing slowed, her heartbeat returned to normal, she stopped shaking, and her thighs stopped feeling like rubber.

Sometime during the moments when she was still floating in her own personal nirvana, Taurin rolled onto his back. He was slick, relaxed, and so gorgeous it made her teeth hurt.

He'd said he loved her. That memory came crashing back. And with it the things he'd told her to think about. She turned her head to look at him. "I love you. I don't mind the dark. And if you make me a vampire, I won't have to watch you stay all young and buff while I shrivel up like a prune. Sure the liquid diet might get a little old, but I bet we could spice it up with a little flavoring. Of course, the idea of drinking blood is a total ick right now, but I suppose once you—"

"No." His voice sounded suddenly tired.

"Excuse me?"

"I won't turn you now. You have to think about it. For a long time. Think about your family. Think about what you'll be giving up." He rubbed his hand across his forehead. "I shouldn't have told you I loved you. I just went with my emotions instead of thinking about you."

She sighed. "I like you big, bad, and bold. Mr. Sensitive doesn't fit you. Let *me* decide what's best for me." Kristin pulled her swimsuit back on and then stood up. "I knocked over my iced tea. Would you go get me some more?" She needed a few minutes of alone time to get her head together. Her heart was already together, so she wasn't worried about that.

He nodded, stood, dressed, and then disappeared around the dune. She stared out at the waves. They looked so cool, and she was so hot and sweaty. She walked down to the water's edge and waded in. This time there was no rip current, and the slap of the waves against her body soothed and excited at the same time.

She was still into her sexual feel-good afterglow, so when the fin sliced the water nearby she almost laughed. Banan must've seen Taurin leave and decided that while the vamp was away the shark would play.

Kristin glanced toward the shore. Banan was standing on the beach peering out at her. He waved.

Oh shit. Swallowing hard, she frantically searched the dark water. There, there, and there. *Three* fins. Something slid past her leg and she screeched. Show her a nose and she'd punch it. Ack, no nose.

She saw Taurin slicing through the water at the same time she heard him in her mind.

"Hold on. Coming. Love you. Kill, kill, kill. Mine!"

Every civilized cell in her body shivered at his in-your-face primitive savagery. And *mine*? What was that about?

But beneath her surface layer of independent butt-kicking modern woman, something much more primal, more elemental wakened.

Her man, er, vampire was racing to her rescue. Lips drawn back to expose deadly fangs, eyes black with bloodlust, Taurin was one scary dude. But he was *her* scary dude.

She barely had time to mutter a "holy cow" before he reached her side. He crouched over her, his eyes actually glowing. *Glowing*, for crying out loud.

Suddenly something grabbed her bikini bottom and swiftly dragged her out into deeper water. Her bikini bottom? Why not her leg? She didn't question as she tried to wiggle out of the piece of material the shark wanted so badly.

Taurin roared his rage and dived underwater. The sea became a foaming cauldron of thrashing bodies. Whatever was holding her bikini let go. She should swim for shore, but no way was she leaving Taurin.

The sound of a motor overhead caught her attention. Glancing up, she saw a huge man balanced on what looked like a flying surfboard. Huh? His shaved head gleamed in the moonlight.

He waved strange-looking weapons in both large hands. Shouting at her, he soared above the water. "Don't be afraid, ma'am, Surfer Guy is on his way." At the last moment, he seemed to lose control of the surfboard. It wobbled and then nosedived into the Gulf.

Kristin would think about how bizarre that was later. Right now, she had a vampire to help. Turning her attention back to the battle raging beneath the surface, she gasped as a thin stream of blood floated to the surface. Oh, God, no!

Just then Taurin broke the surface.

She wrapped herself around him and hung on. "That's it. If we make it to shore alive, you're turning me. Don't try to argue. I've made up my mind. Nothing you say will—"

"Yes." He swam toward shore with her still wrapped around him.

"Change my mind. When I thought I might lose you, I realized a measly seventy or eighty years together would never be enough. I . . ." She frowned as they reached shore, and she finally stood on solid ground. "Did you say *yes*?"

He pulled her into his embrace. "Saffron and Banan are on their way, so I'll say this fast. I thought I wouldn't be in time to save you, and I knew if that happened I'd want to meet the dawn. Huge revelation. I'm a weak man where you're concerned. I don't have the courage to walk away from you. And

I'd never survive watching you grow old and die. So that only leaves one option. But first we get married."

Married? "What a guy. Love the romantic proposal. But the time, the place, and the man are right, so I guess I'll say yes. Besides, I love you too much to quibble over details." Kristin knew her eyes were shiny with tears. "Let's get back to my room so we can celebrate."

She glanced over her shoulder to watch Surfer Guy emerge from the water dragging his surfboard behind him. He wore a triumphant grin as Banan stopped to slap him on the back. Saffron waited impatiently for the backslapping to be over. Good. Surfer Guy had sidetracked them.

Taurin turned to follow her gaze. "That's Deimos. He's the castle's resident action hero."

"Is he . . . ?"

"Don't ask." He led her to their blanket where he picked up her shirt and handed it to her, and then he pulled his T-shirt over his head. Finally he scooped up the blanket.

Just before she left the beach, she rescued his second foil packet from the sand.

She waved it at him. "One more for the celebration."

They stood beside his car for a moment taking a last look at the moon and the waves. He smoothed her hair away from her face. "I love you, Kristin-soon-to-be-Veris. A hundred years from now, I still want to be able to kiss you under a full moon with the sound of waves breaking on the shore."

She stood on tiptoe to brush her lips lightly across his. "I deleted both my articles. Maybe I'll start a hot love story."

Once on their way back to the castle, Kristin thought of something. "What happened to the sharks?"

He shrugged. "I'd like to say I drove them away, but I think Deimos freaked them out."

"Oh."

He smiled at her in the darkness. "And they weren't sharks, sweetheart."

Sparkle drove back to her candy store with three naked weresharks squeezed into the backseat of her car and Deimos filling up the passenger seat next to her.

"You never told us we'd be fighting a pissed-off vampire and the crazy dude sitting next to you." The complaining wereshark looked at his friends and they both nodded their agreement. "The damn vampire took a chunk outta me." His tone turned aggrieved.

Sparkle did a few mental eye-rolls. What a bunch of wusses. "I'll pay you more money, okay?" She parked in back of her store, got out, and handed the weresharks their clothes and extra cash. Then she watched them dress before melting into the darkness.

Deimos stood waiting anxiously beside her. "Did I pass, huh?"

She studied him and then smiled. "You passed. I'm proud of you."

Deimos seemed to swell with pride right in front of her eyes. "That was neat how you hired those weresharks so I'd get a chance to show you my action-hero powers."

"That's what you really want, isn't it?" Time for her to face a truth she'd known for a while.

He nodded eagerly.

"Tell you what I'll do. I'll find a cosmic troublemaker to mentor you who'll give you a little more excitement." Not that she truly believed anything could be more exciting than creating sexual chaos, but a troublemaker who didn't enjoy his work would be a pain in the butt forever. She held up her hand to stop what promised to be an extended string of thank-yous. "Later. Go practice your action-hero moves."

And as she watched him hurry away, she smiled. She wouldn't spoil his joy by telling him that she saved the day for him. Taurin and Kristin needed a close encounter of the deadly kind to shock them into that final commitment.

Damn, she was good. She hummed "Nobody Does It Better" as she let herself into her store.

Turn the page for a preview of

DOUBLE PLAY

By Jill Shalvis

Available July 2009 from Berkley Sensation!

> You spend a good piece of your life gripping a baseball, and in the end it turns out that it was the other way around all the time. —JIM BOUTON

If he had to choose between sex and a nap, he'd have to take the nap, and that was pretty damn pathetic. But Pace Martin's shoulder hurt like a mother and so did his damn pride. The first wasn't new but the second was.

Go home and rest, Pace. That had been his physical therapist's advice.

He'd rest when he was old and closer to dead, he thought as he practically crawled through the clubhouse to his locker. With slow precision, he bent down to untie his cleats, feeling as if he'd been hit with a Mack truck.

This after only thirty minutes of pitching in the bullpen. Thirty minutes doing what he'd been born to do, playing the game that had been his entire life for so long he couldn't remember anything before it, and he felt far closer to old than he wanted to admit. Stripping out of his sweats had him sweating buckets. When he peeled off his T-shirt, spots swam in his eyes. Yeah, look at him; three years as the ace pitcher in the only four-man starting rotation in the majors, now he wanted to whimper like a damn baby. He sagged against his locker and let out a careful breath.

At least no one was here to witness his humiliation—no paparazzi, no press of any kind, none of his Santa Barbara Heat teammates; otherwise, he might have to start a fight just to distract everyone from the fact that he could barely stand.

And that he'd just thrown like complete shit.

Except picking a fight would probably do him in for good, and then he'd need a distraction from that . . . Ah, hell. He eyed the distance to the showers and gritted his teeth. Pushing away from the locker, he made it through the luxurious clubhouse—thank you, Santa Barbara taxpayers—and into the shower room where he caught a glimpse of his reflection in the floor-length mirrors. Stopping to stare had nothing to do with vanity and everything to do with a growing sense of doom. His shoulder was visibly swollen. Not good. Lifting his good hand, he probed at it and hissed out a breath.

Sit out tomorrow's game had been his private doctor's orders. The team doc hadn't gotten a look at him yet, nor had Gage, the Heat's team manager. Hell, he'd even managed to escape Red, his pitching coach, all in the name of not being put on the disabled list. Being DL would give him a required minimum fifteen-day stay out of action.

Yeah. No, thank you. The Heat was nearing the half-way mark of their third season, and as a newbie expansion team notably filled with young players—eighteen out of twenty-five of them had been born in the '80s—they had everything to prove. Three seasons in and anything could happen, even the World Series, *especially* the World Series, and management was all over that.

Hell, the players were all over that. Everyone wanted it so bad they could taste it. But to even get to any postseason play at all, Pace had to pull a miracle, because as everyone loved to obsess over, *he* was the Heat's ticket there. Sure, the team had twenty other pitchers in various degrees of readiness, but none were anywhere close to giving what he gave. Which meant that just about everyone he knew, from the owners down to the very last fan, was counting on him. He was it, baby, the fruition of their dreams.

No pressure or anything.

Reminding himself that he could sit and whine when he was far closer to death than just thirty, he stepped into the shower, rolled his shoulder, and then nearly passed out at the white-hot stab of pain. Holy shit. He was going to need a distraction.

Wild monkey sex. That had been Wade's suggestion. Not surprising, really, given the source. And maybe the Heat's catcher and Pace's best friend was onto something. Too bad Pace didn't want sex, wild monkey or otherwise. And wasn't that just the bitch of it. All he wanted was the game that had been his entire life. He wanted his shot at the World Series before being forced by bad genetics and a loose rotator cuff to quit the only thing that had ever mattered to him.

He didn't have to call his father to find out what the old man would suggest. The Marine drill instructor, the one who routinely terrified soldiers and whose motto was "Have clear objectives at all times," would tell his only son to get the hell over himself and get the hell back in the game before he kicked the hell out of Pace's sorry ass himself for even thinking about slacking off.

And wouldn't that help.

Jesus, now he was pouting. Pace ducked his head beneath the shower and let the hot water pound his abused body until he felt better, because apparently he'd gotten something from his father after all. He had fourteen wins already this season, dammit. He'd thrown twenty-four straight shutout innings. He was having his best season to date; he was on top of his game. The very top—

"Pace? You good?"

Pace shifted so that his shoulder was out of view and under the stream of water as he lifted his head and looked at Gage Pasquel. At thirty-four years old, their "Skipper," as they called him, was the youngest team manager in the country, and possibly the hardest working, a fact that everyone on the Heat wholeheartedly appreciated. Gage was loyal to a fault, calm at all times, and utterly infallible when it came to supporting the Heat in every possible way, including, apparently, coming in on a rare day off.

Just last night they'd all celebrated Skip's birthday at the Playboy mansion, and when Pace had left him at two in the morning, the birthday boy had been fairly impaired, singing charmingly off-key to several exotic bunnies in the grotto.

"I didn't expect to see you up and moving today," Pace told him with a smile he hoped didn't looked like a pain-filled grimace.

"Same goes." Gage had the coloring of his Latin father and the contagious smile of his supermodel mother, the one that got him as many women as any of the guys on the team. But that easygoing, laid-back air hid the temperament of a pit bull. Pace had seen him cut down an ump with a single look, take out an opposing team manager with nothing more than an arched brow, and cower a newbie with a single jab of a finger. And yet when it came to his players, he was more like a momma bear. "Need anything?"

Yeah, a new shoulder would be great. Pace would just put it on his Christmas list. "I'm good." And then prayed that was true.

Gage, not one to pry unless absolutely necessary, nodded and left him alone. Pace took a breath in relief as he washed his hair—not easy with the bad shoulder. When he shook the water out of his eyes, Red stood right on the other side of the tile wall.

"Jesus," Pace muttered. "It's Grand-fucking-Central Station."

The Heat's pitching coach was tall, reed thin, and sported a shock of hair that was both the color of his nickname and streaked with gray that came hard-earned after four decades in the business. He had an old face for his nearly sixty years, thanks to the sun, the stress, and the emphysema he suffered through because he refused to give up either his beloved cigarettes or standing beside the bullpen surrounded by the constant dirt and thick dust.

Red's doctors had been after him to retire for a long time, but like Pace, the guy lived and breathed baseball. He also lived and breathed Pace, going back to their days together at San Diego State. When Pace had landed here with the Heat, Red had followed. Red always followed, which worked for Pace. Red was far more than a coach to Pace, always had been.

All Red wanted was to see the Heat get to the World Series. That's it, and it would kill him to retire before that happened. Knowing it, Pace also knew his arm would have to be falling off before he'd admit any pain to Red and add to his roster of things to worry about.

"What are you doing here?" Red asked in his been-smoking-and-coughing-for-half-a-century voice. "It's a day off. Usually you guys are all over that."

Because they didn't have many. Pace pitched every fourth game, and in between he had a strict practice and work-out schedule. "Maybe I just like the shower here better than my own."

"The hell you do. You throw?"

"A little."

Red's eyes narrowed. "And?"

"And I'm great."

"Your shoulder—"

"What about it?"

"Don't bullshit me, son. You were favoring it yesterday in the pen."

"You need glasses. I'm pitching 2.90, one of the top five in the league right now."

"3.00." Red peered into the shower, all geriatric stealth, trying to get a good look, but Pace had cranked the water up to torch-his-ass hot, and the steam made it difficult to see clearly.

"It's fine." Pace didn't have to fake the irritation. "I'm fine; everything's fine."

"Uh-huh." Red pulled out his phone, no doubt to call in the troops—management—to have Pace's multimillion dollar arm assessed.

It was one of the few cons to hitting the big time—from April to October his time wasn't his own, and neither was his body. Reaching out, water flying, he shut Red's phone. "Relax."

"Relax?" Red shook his head in disbelief. "Are you shitting me? There's no relaxing in baseball!"

Okay, so he had a point. The Heat had done shockingly well their first year, even better their second, gaining momentum as they came out from beneath the radar to gather huge public interest.

With that interest came pressure.

In this, their third year, they were hot, baby, hot, but if they didn't perform, there would be trades and changes. That was the nature of the game. And not just for players.

Red was getting up there and not exactly in the best health. Pace didn't know what would happen if management decided to send Red down to the AA's before he retired on his own terms and walked out with his dignity intact. Well, actually, Pace did know. It would kill him.

And after losing in the playoffs three times in a row prior to coming to the Heat, Pace didn't want another trade. He wanted wins. He was hungry for it. And so was Red, with every agitated, emphysema-ridden breath he took. "Just taking a shower here," Pace assured him. "No hidden agenda." No way was he breaking the guy's big old soft heart. Not yet. Not until he had to.

"Good then." Red coughed, gripped the tile wall, glaring at Pace when he made a move to help. When Red finally managed to stop hacking up a lung, he lay Pace's towel over the tile wall. "I think you've had enough hot water."

"Not yet."

"Your choice, but you're shriveling your junk."

When Pace looked down at himself, Red snorted. "Get out of that hot water, boy."

Boy.

He hadn't been a boy in a damn long time, but he supposed to Red he'd always be a kid. Waiting until Red shuffled away, Pace turned the water off and touched his shoulder. Better, he told himself, and carefully stretched. Good enough.

It had to be.

Because Red had lot at stake. The Pacific Heat had a lot at stake.

And knowing it, Pace had everything at stake.

Holly Hutchins prided herself on her razor-sharp instincts, which hadn't failed her yet—okay, so maybe they routinely failed her when it came to men, but other than that, she always followed her hunches. Following them today had led her to the Pacific Heat's clubhouse, where she waited on one Pace Martin, the celebrated, beloved badass ace starting pitcher she'd just watched in the bullpen.

Not that he knew she'd been observing his closed and clearly very private practice. There'd not been a manager or another player in sight, and certainly no outsiders, including reporters or writers—of which she happened to be both.

She'd sat on the grassy hill high above the Pacific Heat's stadium, surrounded on one side by the Pacific Ocean and on the other by the steep, rugged Santa Ynez mountains. There she'd studied Pace from the shadow of an oak tree.

She hadn't used her camera. Not yet. That would have been an invasion of privacy, and she might be the epitome of a curious reporter, but she had a tight grip on her own personal compass of right and wrong. Taking pictures when he wasn't aware of her even being there would have been wrong.

Which was a shame, because he'd looked fine in his black warm-up sweats and gray Heat T-shirt, his name in flame orange across his broad back. Damn fine. Not a surprise, really, since he was currently gracing the cover of *People* magazine's Most Beautiful People issue.

But what *had* been a surprise—his pitching had sucked.

She'd done her research and knew that didn't happen often, if ever. The baseball phenom was the best of the best. He had three Cy Young awards and two Gold Gloves. He routinely won a minimum of twenty games a season. He had a 3000 ERA last year and was even slightly beneath that this year—an amazing feat. He'd weathered the steroid scandals without a single whisper or hint of being involved.

But in spite of all that, the Heat needed a fantastic year and everyone knew it. The pressure had to be enormous.

She understood pressure. She wrote under enormous pressure. She wasn't a tabloid reporter. Making up tidbits and taking racy pictures didn't turn her on. No, the truth turned her on, *secrets* turned her on, and she was damn good at sniffing out both. Some would say too good. One in particular, rocket scientist Alex Possier, *had* said it, and more.

So she was a tough cookie. So she was determined to get her story no matter what. And so maybe she was a little pushy. So what. She was who she was, and her ex-boyfriend Alex had known that going in.

He'd known it better going out. Besides, he'd been the one on the wrong side of the law—not her.

No regrets.

Reminding herself of that very fact, she looked down at her watch. Dammit. She was on a tight schedule and her phenom was running late. Lateness was rude, an opinion left over from her Southern upbringing, the one she liked to pretend hadn't scarred her—ha!—and she eyed the club-house door, willing him to hurry up.

She hated waiting.

Too bad women were allowed in by invite only—which she had for the upcoming game but not today. If only she had a penis, she could just walk right in and interview him in his element, asking him what the hell had been wrong with him out there today.

Not that she wanted a penis. They were way too much trouble. In fact, given her last fiasco, she'd given up penises.

Or was it peni?

It didn't matter, single or plural, they were a thing of her past. Not a huge loss, as they'd never really done all that much for her except give out brief orgasms and a whole lot of grief.

Her cell rang, and she knew exactly who it'd be. "Hey, Boss."

"You get him yet, Doll?"

Tommy White could have been a man to admire. The *American Living* online editor-in-chief had hired her out of a hundred hopefuls, and she'd never forget that. What she would do is forget how many times he'd asked her to lie, badger an eye witness, or get drunk and sleep with him.

Fact was, he'd given her a weekly blog on his site that had become extremely popular because she picked subjects of national interest, then profiled that subject in depth for three months at a time with an interesting aside—secrets. She'd discovered everyone had one and that people loved to read about them. Her last ongoing series had been on space travel, and she'd won awards for exposing the dangerous use of inferior, cheaper parts, which had resulted in two tragic accidents.

Before that she'd blogged about the ghost towns of the great Wild West, including her own photographs of what had been left behind when those towns had failed. That had ended up getting her a segment on *60 Minutes*.

She was on top of her game, or so everyone said, so why she felt an odd sense of restlessness, she had no idea. She'd thought about taking some time off, but having been born practically in the gutter, doing so felt too luxurious. Besides,

Tommy was nothing if not persistent. So here she was, jumping right into this baseball thing, profiling America's favorite pastime and favorite MLB team for the next few months, figuring she'd just have to get over herself.

She'd thought she'd start easy, focusing her first article toward a personal angle, and she could have picked any of the young, aggressive, charismatic Heat players: Joe Pickler, the second baseman, who had given up medical school to play AA ball and then spent five years working his way up to the majors. Ty Sparks, the relief pitcher who'd overcome childhood leukemia and was trying to work his way up to the starting rotation. Henry Weston, the left fielder turned shortstop, who'd left the Dodgers, where his twin brother played, to join the new Heat in spite of it causing a major family rift. Wade O'Riley, the catcher, by all accounts a happy, affable guy who'd come from abject poverty, something Holly knew all too much about.

A sucker for a challenge, she was starting with Pace, a player three years into his fifty-million-dollar, five-year contract, who'd oddly and very atypically turned down millions more in alcohol and cologne ads, a player the tabloid reporters loved to try to dig up dirt on.

And Tommy's favorite player. "Tell me you got him," he said.

"Not yet."

"What do you mean, he's not there? He stand you up?"

"He's just running a few minutes behind."

Pace hadn't sneaked out on the interview, not with his car still in the parking lot, and as it was a classic candy-apple red Mustang convertible, it was hard to miss. Nope, he was still inside, and she'd get him. She wasn't worried about that. What she was, however, was curious.

Why had he pitched for thirty minutes, punishingly hard in spite of the fact that he'd clearly been having an off day, and then suddenly dropped to the bench, shoulders and head down, breathing as if he'd run a marathon? He'd just sat there, carefully not moving a single inch. Only after many minutes had passed had he pushed to his feet and escaped to the clubhouse.

Was he nursing a heartache?

A hangover?

What?

"He's going to stand you up, Doll," Tommy said sourly.

She'd told him a million times not to call her doll. She'd given up. "He'll come."

And if he'd managed to elude her somehow, she'd figure it out. She was a pro and enjoyed the taste and thrill of the chase, including the adrenaline that rushed through her when the clubhouse door finally opened.

Finally. She hung up on Tommy and hurriedly flashed her friendly, secret-inducing smile just as a tall, dark, and jaw-droppingly gorgeous guy strode out.

Pace Martin in the flesh.

"Hi," she said, gripping her pad of paper and pen, perfectly willing to forgive his tardiness if he made this easy on her. Not that it mattered. They were doing this either way, even if he'd made a secondary career out of being tough, cynical, edgy, and for a bonus, noncommittal. She specialized in tough, cynical, and edgy. She thrust out her hand. "I'm Holly Hut—"

"Sure. No problem." Without making eye contact, he grabbed her pen and leaning over her, quickly wrote something on her pad.

He was in her space now, and she took her first up close look at him, searching for that elusive "it" factor that seemed to make men want to be him and women want to do him. Granted, he owed much of that to his packaging, but she'd already known that. He had wavy dark hair, movie-star dark eyes, and a face directly from the Greek gods, but she wasn't moved by such things. As a writer and a people watcher, Holly knew his pull had to go far deeper, that there was more to his charisma than genetic makeup.

Or so she hoped.

But the charisma sure didn't hurt. His hair was wet from a recent shower. She could smell his shampoo or soap, something woodsy and incredibly male that made her nostrils sort of quiver.

Huh.

Okay, so *People* magazine was right. He did have some genuine sex appeal, she'd give him that. Since she barely came up to his broad shoulders, she had to tip her head up to stare into his face as he handed her back her pad. She had just enough time to see that his eyes weren't the solid brown his bio claimed but had gold swirling in the mix. They weren't smiling to match his mouth, not even close, and if she had to guess, she'd say Mr. Hotshot was pissed at something. Then she glanced down at her pad and saw what he'd done.

He'd signed his name across her pad.

An autograph.

He'd just given her an autograph.

And then, while she was still just staring at the sprawling signature in shock, he handed her back her pen and walked away, heading down the wide hallway.

"Hey," she said. "I didn't want—"

But he'd turned a corner and was already gone.